I0549257

THE CROSS BRAND

Frederick Faust

(Max Brand)

FREDERICK FAUST

THE CROSS BRAND

FREDERICK FAUST, WRITING AS

MAX BRAND

ALTUS PRESS • 2017

© 2017 Altus Press • First Edition—2017

EDITED AND DESIGNED BY
Matthew Moring

PUBLISHING HISTORY
"The Cross Brand" originally appeared in the August 25, 1922 issue of *Short Stories* magazine (Vol. 100, No. 4).

THANKS TO
Everard P. Digges LaTouche

ALL RIGHTS RESERVED
No part of this book may be reproduced or utilized in any form or by any means, electronic or mechanical, without permission in writing from the publisher.

This edition has been marked via subtle changes, so anyone who reprints from this collection is committing a violation of copyright.

Visit altuspress.com for more books like this.

Printed in the United States of America.

CHAPTER I

JACK BRISTOL removed his feet from the table-edge and sat up. It was a tribute of attention which any other man in Arizona would have paid, willingly, to Sheriff Harry Ganton; but what filled the eye of Jack Bristol was not the sheriff's person but the sheriff's horse.

The sight of the brown mare plucked a string in his heart of hearts and filled him with a melancholy of yearning. Such a horse as that could not be bought or bred. She was one of those rare sports which are produced by chance. A grayhound had more speed; a mountain sheep was more nimble climbing the rocks; but brown Susan could imitate both. She was put together with a mathematical nicety, like Jack Bristol's gun, of which she often made him think. But above and beyond physical prowess, it was Susan's personality which delighted Jack. Her starred forehead, her quick-stirring little ears, her great, bright, gentle eyes, and a wise way she had of cocking her head to one side; in short, she fitted nicely into the heart of Jack Bristol and he groaned to think that another man must always ride her.

She came to a stop just in front of the house. The big sheriff dismounted. As he stood beside her, his six feet and odd inches of height, his two hundred pounds of bone and muscle, made her seem hardly more than a pony—in fact she was a scant fifteen three, Jack knew—yet she had carried Ganton prodigious distances between sunrise and dark. She was the foundation upon which his reputation had been raised. Two years before Susan was a tender three year old and Harry Ganton was a newly elected and youthful sheriff. In the past twenty-four months Susan had demonstrated that robbers who committed crimes in the district which Ganton protected were fools if they depended for safety upon the speed of their horses. Brown Susan ran them down with consummate ease, and once she brought Harry Ganton within range he was a known fighter.

The sheriff stepped out of sight and appeared again at the door of the house; Jack Bristol greeted him with a wave of the hand and went to the window where Susan had come to whinny to him with bright eyes of expectancy. He began to slit apples into narrow sectors. She took them daintily from his fingers. The sheriff, in the meantime, took a chair which he could tilt back against the wall.

"Too bad you don't own Sue," he said. "You and her get on uncommon well, Jack."

The head of Jack Bristol jerked around.

"Maybe she's for sale?" he asked. But he sighed and shook his head without waiting for the answer.

"Suppose she were?" said the sheriff. "Would you have the price to spare?"

"I'd find the price," said Jack. He held a glistening bit of apple away, while she reached greedily and vainly for it. "I'd find the price."

"How?" insisted Ganton.

Jack Bristol turned to the other with a peculiarly characteristic air of disdain, as though he were one for whom probabilities had no interest. He was a handsome fellow with lean, clear-cut features and a blue eye which was almost black; and he had a bold and confident glance which now dwelt upon the sheriff with unbearable steadiness. He seemed to have many words on the tip of his tongue, but he only said, "There are ways!"

At this the sheriff shrugged his shoulders. They were of one age, just at thirty; but Jack Bristol looked five years younger and the sheriff seemed in excess of his real age by the same margin. Burdens honorably assumed and patiently borne, fierce labor, honest methods, had marked him with a gray about the forehead and lined his face to sternness or to weariness. But the skin of Jack Bristol was as smooth as the skin of a child.

His eye was as clear. The fingers which poised the fragment of apple above the velvet nose of Susan were as tapered as the fingers of a woman. Labor had never misshaped that hand or calloused it. The sheriff marked these things with a touch of bitterness. They had gone to the same school at the same time. He had fought his way through the studies. Jack Bristol, never opening a book, the hours of his bright leisure never encroached upon, had always led the class. Now, so many years later, it mattered not that Ganton could savagely assure himself of his success and Jack's failure. The instant he came into the presence of the latter, he felt his crushing inferiority.

"There are ways, eh?" echoed Ganton. "But how, Jack? The cards?"

This time Jack Bristol turned his back squarely upon the mare, though one hand, behind him, continued to pat her.

"What the devil do you mean by that?" he asked.

"I mean that everybody in town knows how you've kept your head up," answered the sheriff. "We know that you're a fat one with the cards!"

"A crooked gambler, eh?"

"I haven't said that. I think you'd be honest at it."

"Thank you."

"Simply because you're too proud to admit that another man might have better luck than you."

"What the devil ails you, Ganton? What do you mean by coming here with this sort of talk? What have I and my ways to do with you? Have you turned sky-pilot, maybe? Going to try for two jobs at once?"

The sheriff flushed.

"I'll tell you why I've come. I've always kept out of your way—"

"Because you had nothing on me!"

"Maybe. I say, I've never bothered you until you mixed up with my business. Then I had to let you know that I was around."

"In your business?"

"Last week you went to Hemingworth to the dance in the schoolhouse, didn't you?"

Jack Bristol was again half turned away, paying far more attention to the feeding of the mare than to the words of the sheriff. But Ganton persisted in his questions in spite of this insulting demeanor.

"I suppose I did," nodded Jack. "I've forgotten."

"Forgotten! That's the place where you met Maude Purcell and danced half the dances with her and made her town talk next day and ever since."

"Maude Purcell? I remember that name."

"I guess you do!"

"She's a girl with pale eyes and freckles across her nose. Kind of cross-eyed, too, isn't she?"

He spoke carelessly, busy with the feeding of Susan. But from the corner of his eye he saw the sheriff writhe and it gave him a malicious pleasure.

"I can't let you talk like that," burst out the sheriff. "Jack, you didn't know or else not even you would of dared to talk like this, but me and Maude are engaged to get married!"

"You are?" said Jack. First he gave the last of the apple to the mare. Then he took out a handkerchief and began to wipe his fingers. Last of all, he turned to the sheriff. "Of course," he said, "in that case I'm mighty sorry, Harry. Wouldn't have hurt your feelings for the world!"

The sheriff, very red of face, watched him narrowly, and sighed. He had a perfect conviction that Jack Bristol knew all about his relations with pretty Maude Purcell. He was reasonably sure that it was on this very account that Jack had flirted so outrageously with Maude on that evening. But Bristol was no man to force into a corner; it would not do to anger him unless that were a last resource.

"What I mean," said the sheriff, "is this: Maude and me *were* engaged. But—the other day we busted it off!"

Jack started. He flashed at the sheriff a glance of real concern, but the latter was looking down in anguish to the floor and when he raised his head again, Jack had succeeded in smoothing his expression to indifference.

"She gave me over," said the sheriff again. He mopped his forehead. "And the reason she done it was because—because of the way you talked to her that night at the dance! That's why I've come here to talk to you, Jack!"

Jack Bristol looked back into his mind in dismay. Maude Purcell, on that night, with her yellow hair and blue dress and gay smile, had been the prettiest girl on the dance floor. Also, she gained piquancy through Jack's knowledge that she was the bride-to-be of the sheriff. He and Harry Ganton were old enemies. They were the bywords of the town. He was the example of riotous living and idleness held up to the youth of the community. Harry Ganton was the example of what a young man may accomplish by industry and frugal living. It had been a shrewd temptation to win the girl away from thoughts of her lover for a single evening. But to lead to this result certainly had never been in his mind.

"And the first thing I got to ask," said the sheriff, "is this: what sort of intentions have you got toward Maude?"

Jack Bristol had been on the verge of stepping across the room, shaking the hand of Harry with an apology for his conduct, and promising his best assistance in smoothing out the tangle. But the stern voice of the sheriff threw him back into another mood at once. He could never be driven with whips where he might be led by the slightest crooking of a finger. In fact, the humor of Jack was generally that of a spoiled boy.

"Are you her father?" asked Jack. "Where's your right to ask me what my intentions are?"

"I got the right of a man whose happiness is tied up in what you may do!" exclaimed poor Ganton, turning pale with emotion.

"Well, Harry, I haven't made up my mind!"

"Then, gimme a chance to help you make it up!"

"Go as far as you like."

"In the first place, are you the sort that makes a marrying man?"

"How d'you mean by that?"

"Ain't a man, if he's going to marry, got to be the sort that will provide a home for his wife and enough for her and their kids to live on?"

"You think I couldn't do that?"

"You could do it plumb easy. That ain't the thing. Would you do it? Wouldn't you get tired of the house and everything in it? Wouldn't you want a change? Ain't that the way you've been all the rest of your life?"

"Maybe it is."

"It's a sure enough fact. Look around here at this house. Why, I can remember on the day your father died, this was the best house in Red Bend. We all used to look up to it. It was the sort of a house that we all wanted to build and live in some day if we ever got to be that rich. And look at the house now! Look where the rain has leaked in through the roof that you ain't ever repaired; see where it's streaked and stained the walls! Look where the wallpaper is beginning to peel off and where it's faded. The flooring is all in waves in your big dining-room. You've sold all the good furniture. You've got only a bunch of junk left. The roof of your big barn is busted and sagging in. Your cows have been sold down to just a few dozen. You only got a couple of hosses. You've loaded your ranch up to the ears with mortgages. And now I ask you, Jack, to stand back and look at things fair and square, including yourself. After you've had a good look, tell me if you're the kind that makes a family happy. Are you?"

Against his will, Jack Bristol had been forced to follow the eager words of the sheriff. The unhappy picture was painted in vivid strokes, and out of his memory was drawn the coloring for it. All the prosperity of his youth floated past him like a tantalizing vision. Behind it was the face of his father, that too-indulgent man.

It is when we feel our guilt too keenly that we are most apt to anger. Also, no doubt the sheriff had paid more attention to truth than to tact.

"Ganton," said Jack. "I'm glad to know what you think of me. But it don't follow that that's what I think of myself. As for the girl, if she got tired of you I'm sorry for you, but maybe she figures it shows she has sense. We all have a right to our opinions, eh?"

The sheriff changed color again. But he kept himself strongly under control.

"You're hot-headed now, Jack. But I know that you ain't as hard as all that. You ain't going to keep up your game with Maude just for the sake of putting me in the fire, eh?"

"What game?" said Jack. "Suppose that Maude and I should

decide to step off together? What then? Why shouldn't we marry?"

"Why?" echoed the sheriff, looking wildly about him. "Jack, you don't mean it!"

"Is there any law on your side to stop us?" asked the other cruelly.

"There is," said the sheriff, and he rose from his chair.

"Name it, partner!"

"It's this."

The sheriff tapped the gun hanging at his side.

"I'll put an end to you first, Bristol. I've seen you spoil everything you've touched. I ain't going to see you spoil her face—not while I'm wearing a gun!"

Jack Bristol gasped, as one immensely surprised. Anger followed more slowly. "You damned blockhead!" he fumbled for words. "Stop me with a gun—me?"

His right hand trembled down to his own weapon and came away again. He whipped out Bull Durham and brown papers and rolled himself a smoke which he lighted and walked hurriedly up and down the room, a wisp of smoke following him and banking up into a little cloud when he turned.

"Get out, Harry!" he implored the sheriff. "Get out before something happens. I know you're a good fighter. Everybody around these parts thinks that you can't be beat. But you know and I know that I'm faster and straighter with a gun. I dunno what's got into your crazy head. Are you hunting for a way to die?"

"It don't make no difference," said the sheriff. "I've come here to make you promise that you'd give up Maude. If I couldn't persuade you to do it, I was going to make you. And that goes! I'd rather see you dead and me hanging for the murder than to have Maude's life ruined. What are both of our lives compared with hers?"

"Harry, go home and think it over," said Jack Bristol. "You

ain't talking sense. You know you can't budge me. You ain't man enough. You never were!"

"Answer me one way or the other, Jack. Will you give her up? You know that even if you had her you couldn't be true to her. You ain't made that way. All your life the girls have talked soft to you. You've had your way paved with smiles. They don't mean nothing to you. Maude would be getting the first wrinkles before long. And then you'd be through with her. I know how it'd be. You'd leave her. You've never stuck to the same girl for a whole summer. Ain't that a fact? So I ask you—will you give her up?"

"I'll see you damned first!"

"Then God help one of us!"

He pitched himself to one side while a swift flexion of hand and wrist brought out the Colt. It began spitting fire and ploughing the floor with lead. The first bullet split a board at the feet of Jack Bristol. The second, as the gun was raised, was sure to drive into the body of Jack himself. But before that second shot a forty-five calibre slug struck the sheriff in the breast and knocked him against the wall.

He recoiled, gasping, fired from a wobbling hand a bullet that tore upward through the roof, and then dropped upon his face.

CHAPTER II

THAT IMPACT forced up on either side of the body a puff of dust, which was deep on the floor. Before the little clouds settled, Jack Bristol was beside the prostrate man and had jerked him over to his back. There was a deep gash across his forehead where he had struck the floor. Blood was hot and thick on the breast of his coat. Jack kneeled, fumbled for the pulse, felt none, and sprang up again to flee for his life.

Down the street men were calling. He heard them with wonderful clearness.

"Hey, Billy, come in! There's hell popping up at—"

"I'm coming. Where's Jordan? Hey, Pop, we've got to get—"

"Run, boys. There's enough of us!"

But still they clamored as they swept slowly up the street. No, they were not moving slowly. They were only slow by comparison with the leaping speed with which the brain of Jack Bristol was considering possibilities.

Should he stay to demand his trial as a man fighting in self-defense? No, that would never do; he could hear beforehand the roar of angry mirth with which Red Bend would hear of this plea from Jack Bristol, gambler from time to time, spendthrift on all occasions while the money lasted, and gun-fighter extraordinary. No, he must never dream of standing his ground. His first difficulty would be to find a fast horse. His gray gelding was fast enough to escape most pursuit, but the gray was in a distant pasture. But why should he worry about getting a fast horse when brown Susan herself stood just outside his window? And why not be hunted for horse-stealing as well as murder?

He was out of the window as that thought half formed. Susan drew back, but only a step. He whipped into the saddle with half a dozen men plunging toward him, the leaders not fifty yards away, with the liquid dust spurting up around their feet. He had known those men all his life. But now they went at him like town-dogs at a wolf, yelling, "He's got Harry—he's dropped the sheriff—shoot the hound!"

Jack Bristol sent Sue into a racing gallop with a single word. In an instant he had twitched her around the corner of the house with a flight of bullets singing behind her. She took a high fence flying. She sprinted across a cleared space beyond. She winged her way across a second fence and was hopelessly out of range for effective revolver shooting before the pursuers reached the corner of the house. So they tumbled into the house, instead of continuing, and there they found the sheriff, dripping with blood, in the act of rising from the floor.

"Leave Jack alone!" were his first words. "I'm not killed. I brung this on myself. He glanced a chunk of lead along my ribs, and I deserved it! Get Doc Chisholm, boys!"

"But Jack has grabbed Susan!"

Here the sheriff groaned, but almost at once he controlled himself and answered, "Then let him take her till he finds out that he ain't wanted here. All I hope to God is that he don't turn desperado because he thinks that he's done one killing already."

Of course Jack Bristol could not know it, but that was the reason there was no pursuit. He himself attributed it to the known speed of brown Susan. The good citizens of Red Bend knew enough about her not to expect to run her down in a straight chase; only by maneuver and adroit laying of traps could they expect to capture the man who bestrode her. Such was the reason to which Jack Bristol attributed the failure of any pursuit, though, as a matter of fact, Sheriff Ganton was sending out hasty messages in all directions striving to head off the fugitive and let him know that the law had no claim against him. It was all the easier for the sheriff to send those messages because, that night, Maude Purcell sat by his bed to nurse him. The more brilliant and dashing figure of Jack Bristol might have turned her head for the instant, but when she heard of the wounding of Harry Ganton all doubt was dissolved. A voice spoke out of her heart and drove her to the sheriff's side.

But that night Jack Bristol squatted beside the thin and wavering smoke of his camp-fire and peered from his hilltop into the desert horizon with the feeling that the hostility of the world encompassed him with full as perfect and unbroken a circle. And in truth it was not altogether an unpleasant sensation. It was a test of strength, and he had plenty of that. He stretched his arms and felt the long muscles give with a quiver. Yes, he had plenty of strength. He felt, also, that for the first time he was playing the rôle for which he was intended. He was no producer. He was simply a consumer. He was framed by nature to take, not to make. He was equipped with an eye which saw more surely, a hand which struck more quickly, a soul without dread of others. And all his life he had felt that law was a burden not made for him to carry.

Now the band was snapped and as a first fruit of his labor—behold brown Susan! He turned with a word. The mare came to him like a dog. She regarded him with glistening, affectionate eyes until a cloud of smoke filled her nostrils. She snorted the smoke out and retreated. But still, from the little distance, she regarded him with pricking ears. He had known her since she was a foal. He had loved her from the first as a miracle of horse-flesh. Harry Ganton, consenting to his plea, had allowed him to break the filly in her third year. And now, in her fifth, what wonder was it that she obeyed him almost by instinct. The sheriff had been like an interloper upon her back. Here was her true master! And was it not worth while to be guilty of a theft when stealing brought such a reward as this?

In a sort of ecstasy, Jack Bristol sprang up and began pacing up and down. They would never catch him, now that he had brown Susan. No doubt they were laying their traps, even now. But their traps would never catch him. Other men, weaker men, after they committed their crimes, were sure to circle back to their home towns sooner or later. But he would prove the exception. There were no ties of a sufficient strength to make him return. No, he would lay a course straight to the north and strike a thousand miles into the mountains.

HE LIVED up to the letter of that resolution. For the three following days he pressed on at great speed to outstrip the first rush of the pursuit. At the end of that time he struck a more steady and easy gait and every stage of the journey brought him further and further on the journey north. During the first week, if he had gone into any town, he would probably have found news which would have made him return on his tracks. But he avoided all towns, and soon he was in a strange land to which the following messages of honest Harry Ganton never extended.

So the day at last came, far, far north in the Rockies, when he decided that he must have come into a new land where no one could have heard of him. Brown Susan had just topped a great height. From the shoulder of the mountain they saw a host of smaller peaks marching away in ridge on ridge to the farther north, all as sharp as waves which a storm has whipped up to points. Heavy forest filled the hollows and the lower stretches. It thinned as it climbed, until it came to the desert at timberline.

From that point of vantage, it seemed an eternity of mountains. They seemed to roll out in all directions to the end of the world. It was sunset time. The summits were bright; the lowlands were already black. And Jack Bristol, born and bred to the open of the flat desert, shuddered a little before he allowed Susan to lurch onto the downslope.

All strange country is apt to be terrible. This prospect chilled the man from the desert to the very heart. But he reassured himself. He had lived on the country through a thousand mile trip. He had not spent a cent. On one occasion he had slipped into an outlying ranch-house and stolen an ample supply of ammunition. Otherwise he had not needed the assistance of men. Neither had brown Susan. She had the lines of an Arab; but she had the incredible durability of a mustang. Now she was a trifle gaunt of belly, her forward ribs were showing, but her head was as high, her eye as bright, her tail as arched as when she began the long journey. If horse and rider could survive what they had survived, there was surely nothing to concern them even in a forest wilderness. Where there were living trees other things must live also.

But when they reached the bottom of the slope, Susan going with goat-footed agility among the rocks, and the damp, thick shadow of premature night closed above their heads. Jack Bristol cursed softly, and it seemed to him that half of the high spirit went out of the mare at the same instant. She went timorously on. A great roaring grew out at them from the right. It turned into the distinguishable dashing of a waterfall. And this, in turn, struck out a thousand varying echoes from cliffs and steep hillsides, so that noises continually played around them. Next, they entered a blackness of a great forest. They made their way, not by light, but by distinguishing shadows among shadows. And the penetrating dampness was like an accumulating weight upon the spirit of Jack Bristol.

The way at length began to pitch up again. The trees grew more sparse. And presently, opening into a pleasant clearing, he found himself face to face with a little cabin. It was made of logs, but it was quite pretentious in size. Rather than use up any of the arable land in the level space below it, and on account of which, no doubt, it had been built, the cabin stood among the rocks of the farther slope, leaning back to keep from a fall. Altogether, it seemed to Jack Bristol the most beautiful dwelling he had ever looked upon.

A horse neighed from a small pasture near the house. Susan quivered on the verge of replying, but a sharp slap on the flank made her shake her head and change her mind with a soft little grunt. In the meantime, from his place of secure shadow, Jack watched the smoke rise straight above the stovepipe until it reached a region of greater light. The smoke column, for mysterious reasons, was an assurance that kindly people inhabited the house. To be sure, it would be better to go on, but when the wind carried a faint scent of frying bacon to the nostrils of Bristol, he gave way.

He crossed the clearing. Without dismounting, he leaned from the saddle and tapped at the door. It was opened by a bald-headed man with a Roman nose and a great mass of dirty-gray beard. His sleeves were rolled up over hairy forearms. In one hand he carried a great butcher knife, greasy and steaming.

"Howdy," said Jack Bristol. "Have you got room for an extra man tonight?"

"Howdy, stranger," said the man of the log cabin. He paused while he surveyed Jack keenly. "I reckon I might."

CHAPTER III

WHEN HE came in, carrying his bridle and the saddle heavy with his pack, he found that the interior of the cabin was less in keeping with its exterior and more in keeping with the appearance of the big man of the bald head. For there was a great deal of dirt and confusion and darkness. The cabin had been laid out and built upon a most pretentious scale as though there had been any quantity of muscle and ax-power available at the time of its construction. Besides this big central room, there was another room at each end of the house, though apparently these apartments were now of use merely as junk rooms.

It was plain, at a glance, that a number of men, and only men, lived here. No woman could have endured such confusion for an instant. Guns, harness, old clothes in varying stages of dirt and decay, rusted spurs, broken knives, homemade furniture, shattered by ill usage, littered the floor or hung from pegs along the wall. Every corner was a junk heap. The useable space on the floor was an ellipse framed with refuse. No one who lived in this adobe had ever thought of throwing things away. What was broken lay where it fell until it was kicked from under foot and landed crashing against the wall.

Jack went into the room at the western end of the house and cleared a space to lay down his blankets. Then he returned to the host who was in the act of dropping more wood into the stove. As he did so, the red flame leaped, and by that light he saw the mountaineer more clearly. The skin of his face glistened as though coated with a continual perspiration, in all the places where the beard did not grow. But the beard came up high on the cheeks and was only trimmed, one could see, where it threatened to get in the way by becoming too long. To ward against that, it was chopped off square a few inches below the chin. And it thrust straight out in a wiry tangle.

The outthrust of the beard completed the regularity of the facial angle. The slope carried up from the beard along the hooked nose, and from the nose along a narrow, sharply slanted forehead. In the middle of that forehead was a peculiar scar in the form of a roughly made cross. Jack had not seen it at first, but when the fire leaped, the scar glistened white and was plainly visible.

Altogether he was an ugly fellow, and his ugliness was summed up in a pair of eyes which, considering the great length of the face and the great bulk of the body, were amazingly small. When Jack came closer, he noted a peculiar freak about those eyes. The beard was chiefly gray and dirt in color. But once it must have been a rich red. And the eyelashes, which were of remarkable length, were still of the original deep red, unfaded to their very tips. So that when he squinted it was almost as though he were looking out of reddish eyes.

He was squinting now, as he looked across at Jack Bristol.

"A hoss like that one you ride—a man must be pretty interested in traveling fast to want a hoss like that," observed the mountaineer.

"Maybe," said Jack, and as he spoke he went to the back door of the house, opened it, and whistled. At once brown Susan whinneyed in answer. During their three weeks on the road they had grown wonderfully intimate, wonderfully in accord.

The man of the cabin marked this interchange of calls with a gaping interest.

"Might be a circus hoss, to be as smart as that!" he suggested.

"Might be," answered Jack Bristol.

His reluctance to talk brought a scowl from the other. The big man shifted his weight from one foot to the other, widening the distance between his feet, and hitched his trousers higher. They were secured with a heavy canvas belt, drawn extremely tight. For, in spite of his fifty odd years of age, the man of the cabin was as gaunt-waisted as a youth. He was almost as agile, also, in his movements around the cabin, stepping with the gliding ease of a young athlete. Jack Bristol watched him with a growing aversion. He could not talk to such a great beast of a man, but since he was about to accept the hospitality of the fellow he was ill at ease.

Supper, however, was now ready. They ate boiled potatoes, half seared bacon, stale corn pone, and coffee which was an impenetrable and inky black. And while they ate, on either side of the rough-hewn plank laid on sawbucks which served as a table, they spoke not a word. Jack Bristol rallied himself once or twice to speak, but on each occasion his voice failed him—for when he lifted his glance he never failed to be startled and awed by the red-tinted eyes of the man of the mountains.

Afterward, Jack retired to the pasture, saw that all was well with the mare, and then came in to his blankets. He had barely turned himself in them when he was soundly asleep.

That sleep was broken up by a crashing fall. He sat up and found that the door to his sleeping room was dimly outlined with light, but after the noise there was no sound. A sudden fear gripped Jack Bristol. He realized, in fact, that all his nerves were on edge, for in his sleep he had dreamed of the man of the bald head and the red-fringed eyes, and the dream had been a horror. He stole to the door, and lying down flat on his side, he found that he was able to look into the larger room, and there he saw not one, but two men. The one was his host of earlier in the evening. The other was a younger man, who was also less bulky. The lower half of his face was shrouded, like that of the elder man, with dense beard, save that in his case the beard was of jetty black. They sat now with their heads raised, in the attitude of people listening. The stranger was in the act of finishing a meal. His right hand still surrounded his tin coffee cup. His left hand shoved back his plate.

Presently he shrugged his shoulders, leaned, picked up from the floor another tin plate, whose fall had apparently caused the racket. They conversed for a moment, now, in murmuring voices, not a syllable of which reached the understanding of Jack Bristol. But he had seen and heard enough to alarm him seriously. The fall of a plate would not have been enough to freeze them into such attitudes as he had discovered them in if their minds had been innocently employed. And neither would it be necessary for them to lower their voices so much now. Certainly it was not mere consideration for the sleeping guest which controlled them.

The younger man was now talking eagerly, with many gestures, while the other listened with a scowl so black that the shining scar on his forehead quite disappeared. He shook his head violently from time to time, but the younger still insisted and finally seemed to beat down the resistance of him of the bald head. He half rose. He swept his right hand through a curving, horizontal line in the air, then, with both hands he gestured down. And it came sharply home to Jack Bristol that they were talking about a horse. They were talking about a horse and therefore they must be talking about Susan. For who could speak of any other when brown Susan was near?

The conclusion they reached was now patent. They started up from the table of one accord. Once the elder man was persuaded, he was completely of the youngster's mind. He caught up from the table a long revolver which had been lying there while they talked. The youth produced two weapons of the same sort, and side by side they strode softly down the room and straight toward the door behind which Jack Bristol lay. But the revolvers were not the chief center of his interest. That upon which his gaze fastened was the forehead of the youth which, when the latter turned toward the door, displayed upon it a great glistening scar in the shape of a cross!

For a moment Jack could not stir. Even noticed at random upon the face of one man, that scar had been a grisly and forbidding thing, but seen on another it was increased a thousand fold in interest. It became a horror. It was a human brand, and certainly there was a grim story behind it. What was of first importance to Jack was that men who were forced to bear this grisly mark of identification in their foreheads would be capable of any sort of action.

He himself rose to his feet, stepped back to his blankets, found his cartridge belt, and drew forth the long revolver which hung in a holster attached to it. So armed, he stole on to the window, but when he came closer to it he saw that he could not attempt to leave in that manner. It was so narrow that he was almost sure to be wedged in it. And if he were he would be at the mercy of the others.

Before he could make a more careful examination, the door to the main room opened and the two entered, the younger man walking first with both of his weapons raised and his shadow lunging before him. He leaned over the blankets, then straightened with a gasp.

"Dad, he's gone!"

The instant he lowered his guns, as he spoke, Jack Bristol sprang forward. He had no will to fight them both in those cramped quarters. Either, by himself, would have been more than enough to engage a hardy man. Together, they made tremendous odds. As he leaped in, Jack aimed and drew the trigger. But instead of an explosion and a bullet driven into the body of Black-beard, there was only a loud click and a hollow jar of the hammer descending upon an empty chamber. His gun had been emptied before the attack was undertaken.

Black-beard whirled with a short cry, both guns blazing, and Jack sprang to the side. A bullet stung his side—a mere clipping of the skin. Before him loomed the two-gun man with weapons leveled and not two yards between them. Jack dropped to his knees as the guns roared in unison. The flash had been in his very eyes; the scent of powder was choking and stinging in his throat. Half-blinded, he dived in toward the legs of the other. His shoulders struck beneath the knees. Down upon him toppled the mountaineer with a yell of alarm.

They whirled into a tangle of clutching, striking hands and twining legs. In the background, Jack saw the bald-headed man stepping swiftly about, striving to get in a blow or a shot, but never able to secure a chance without endangering his son. Strong fingers caught at Jack's throat. He beat the hand away, the finger tips tearing into the flesh like hot irons. And as they whirled again he caught at the flash of the revolver which Black-beard still held, jerked it down, and strove to tear it away. The gun exploded. Black-beard sank in a limp heap, and Jack Bristol stood up with an effective weapon in his hand.

He stood up with the roar of the father ringing in his ears and a storm of bullets pouring toward him. He raised the gun to answer that outburst of fire and lead, but he was struck on the head a blow that knocked the flash of the mountaineer's exploding Colt into a thousand sparks. He toppled back into a sea of fire that did not burn.

CHAPTER IV

HE WAKENED with a grip of rope stinging his wrists. There was a bandage around his head. His face and neck and shirt were still wet from the water with which his wound had been washed. Above him were the stars. He was seated upon the damp ground, his shoulders resting against the log wall of the cabin.

His brain noted these changes in swift succession. Then a shadow crept over him. It was the shadow of a man swinging up and down across the shadow of a lantern as he dug with a spade in the dirt. The silhouette grew more living as his senses returned. All at once he recognized the face and the bulky body of the father. He stood in a hole which was already almost hip deep, and it was sinking rapidly. At the edge of the growing heap of dirt which the laboring spadesman threw out, lay a limp form, with the pale glimmer of the forehead turned up to the sky and the lower part of the face lost in the black shadow of a beard.

And Jack knew that he was watching the burial of the son by the father. He himself had been dragged out there for what end? To be buried alive with the dead body of the boy? There was no brutality, he felt, which was past the capacity of the man of the bald head. The care with which his head had been bandaged might augur a more terrible torment for which he was being saved.

He moved his legs. The feet, he found, were tied together as fast as the hands, and he was utterly helpless.

In the meantime, the hole sank with astonishing rapidity to the midsection, the shoulders, and the head of the digger. Finally there was only the grinding of the spade against stones, now and then, and the briefly seen shadow of the spade as it swung up above the mound of dirt for an instant. Then the big man climbed out and stood mopping his forehead and neck with a handkerchief. He was breathing heavily, and when he put away the handkerchief, he turned, leaning upon the spade, and peered into the depths of the hole he had just finished digging.

"That ain't bad," he said at length. "That ain't bad work—not for me getting old. Hello!"

Jack had neither stirred nor spoken, but with this exclamation, the mountaineer wheeled about and strode up to his captive. Propping his hands against his knees, he leaned over and stared into the face of Jack.

"Wide awake and feeling fine, eh?" he suggested. His cheerfulness made Jack shudder. He returned no answer.

"Wide awake and feeling fine," repeated the other, as though a proper reply had been made. "That's as it should be."

He turned again, lifted the body beside the dirt mound, climbed the heap and disappeared into the shadow beyond. After a little time, he reappeared, and stood for some time at the verge of the grave, buried in thought. The place was so profoundly quiet that Jack could hear the rustling of the leaves blown to him from the far side of the clearing, swishing and crisping together like silk skirts on dancers.

And with every moment the horror increased. The big man came back to him, touched the rope which bound his feet with a knife, and then helped him strongly to his feet. He was led in silence to the edge of the grave. The mountaineer held up the lantern until the light fell upon the pale young bearded face within the shadow, glistening on the cross which marked his forehead.

"What I ask you man to man, stranger," said the older man, "is: D'you think when God sees him like that, he'll bear any malice for what he's done? What d'you think?"

The certainty that he had to do with a madman swept over Jack, but while his blood was freezing in the first shock of that conviction, the other went on to quietly answer his own question.

"No, there ain't going to be no malice borne. Look at the chance that he had? It wasn't no chance at all!"

He dropped a heavy hand upon the shoulder of Jack.

"Him down there," said the mountaineer, "was the youngster of the lot. His beard came out blacker'n hell. But he ain't no more'n twenty-two. Look how white his face is! The sun didn't have no time to burn him brown. He was the youngster of the four, and he was worth the other three. If it come to walking, running, riding, shooting, there wasn't a one of 'em that could touch him. I seen a time when he wasn't more'n fifteen and the rest of us got nothing but snow off the mountains. Out would go Charlie. No matter what kind of weather. That wouldn't stop him. And he'd come back with a mess of partridge—a meal of something. I seen a time when he was sick. The rest of us done the hunting for a week. We got nothing; nothing to speak of, that is. Charlie gets up from his bunk. He goes out. It was along in the first black of the evening. Two minutes after he started we heard his rifle working. We run out, and right yonder on the far side of the clearing we seen him standing over a bear that he'd just drilled clean. And when we come up we seen that the foam from the bear's mouth was slavered all over Charlie's boots. That's the sort of nerve he had even when he was a kid. He just stood up and kept pumping lead into the bear till the varmint dropped in the nick of time. That's the sort that Charlie was!"

He dragged off his battered hat and looked up.

"If I'd had ten wives instead of one and all of the ten had four sons, there wouldn't of been another Charlie! And he was enough to of got back at the rest of 'em for me! He'd of made 'em get down and crawl in the end—damn them, damn them to hell!"

He uttered the last words with a quiet savagery. His voice did not rise, but his whole big body shook with his rage.

"Well," he said finally, "that's finished! I take my luck the way I find it. Charlie's gone. I'll find some other way of getting back at 'em!"

He turned upon Jack a baleful glance.

"Get back over yonder," he said. "Don't try no running away. You got your hands tied behind you, and that way you couldn't run fast enough to keep away from me. And if I caught you, I'd make you think that hell was a church party compared to what I'd do to you!"

He spoke these violent words in a voice of no more than conversational loudness but they were more convincing to Jack than if they had been shouted at his ear. He obeyed the order and stood quietly while the other shoved and scooped the great mound of soft dirt into the grave. When it was ended he stepped to the side of the clearing, stooped and then returned staggering under the weight of an immense rock which, when dropped upon the mound, sank half its diameter into the soft earth. The father kept up the labor until he had covered the grave of his son with a great heap of boulders. At length he stepped back, filled a pipe, and while he lighted it, looked with great complacence upon his work.

"Take it by and large," he said, "it would be considerable wolf that could dig down under them rocks, eh?"

He chuckled softly, then turned his back upon that scene and escorted Jack to the house. Here he hung the smoky lantern on a high peg, motioned Jack to a seat on one of the stools which served the place instead of chairs, and, since the night was growing rapidly cold, kindled a brisk fire in the stove. The draught roared up the chimney and set the flimsy stovepipe shaking and softly rattling. The glow of warmth spread. Above it floated the wide drift of the mountaineer's pipe smoke.

"Speaking by and large," he said, "a man might say that no good comes out of fine looking hosses. They's only one thing that racing is good for, and that's for the hosses that does the running. Them that own the hosses go to hell. I've seen 'em start. I've seen 'em finish."

He delivered this little series of moralities without looking at Jack in a fashion which was peculiarly his own, canting his head and gesturing toward Jack, while he faced quite another point in the compass.

Jack found no reply which he could make. So he waited, and all the while his eager, restless eyes went up and down the strong body and the unhuman face of the other. He was striving to solve a riddle and meeting with no success. The big man now picked up a poker and inserted it into the fire under one of the top covers of the stove.

"You think," said Jack at last, "that I'm going to make a fuss about what's happened. But that ain't what's in my mind. Fact is, I'm glad enough to be up and kicking. I'll give you my word that you'll hear no more of me the minute I get my hands free. Or, better still, keep my hands tied, let me get on the back of my hoss, and then turn us loose. How does that strike you?"

The other smoked steadily and gravely throughout Jack Bristol's speech. He regarded his captive with the most profound attention, wrinkling his brows until the scar, as usual, went out of sight.

"I suppose maybe that sounds like the right thing for you to do," he said at length, "but I got something else figured out. You wouldn't see the why of it if I was to tell you. But a gent needs patience to get on any place. A gent needs a pile of patience. And I'm a patient man! After they done their trick with me, I come up here with my family. Anybody else would have tried to get back at 'em one by one, right away. But I didn't do that. I waited. I come up here where there was nobody else, and

I waited and waited for my boys to grow up. They growed up strong and straight, and every one of 'em was a hard fighter, and a good shot. But I lost the three of 'em by hard luck. And still I had Charlie, that's worth all the other three.

"D'you think that I turned Charlie loose on 'em then? No, partner, I didn't. I kept him here all quiet. He was wise enough and quick enough to of gone down at 'em like a wolf. But I waited and waited. I'd get him bigger and stronger. I'd get him quicker still with a gun. And then I'd give him a list of 'em and turn him loose. That was what I was waiting so patient for. I've waited more'n twenty years for it. And at the end of the twenty years, just when Charlie is about to be sprung on 'em, along you come, all made up of hell-fire and claws. And yonder is my twenty years of hoping and waiting a-lying in the ground."

At the conclusion of this long speech, during all of which he had failed to meet the eye of Jack for a single instant, he rose from his chair.

"What I been saying," he said, "you mostly don't understand right now. But you'll know more about in a year from now."

Jack Bristol drew a longer breath. Whatever devilry might be stirring through the strange brain of this man, at least he did not intend murder.

"A year from now," continued the mountaineer, "you'll be riding your hoss around these hills and then you'll understand everything that I been saying now. And I got patience enough to wait till then." So saying, he stepped to the side of the room, took down a length of rope, and with it approached his victim.

There was no possible purpose to be gained by resistance. Jack submitted while he was trussed hand and foot, so that he could not move. Even his head was lashed into a rigid position against a stake which was passed down his back. With this done, the other stepped back, regarded Jack for a critical moment, then went to the stove and took from it the poker.

The fire had turned the end of the iron rod into a living thing. It pulsed with heat. Light waves ran up and down it. It snapped

sparks to a distance, and it cast a white radiance over the slant-
ing face of the mountaineer.

The first premonition as to his purpose struck through Jack
Bristol. Yet he could not believe. It was only when the big man
advanced squarely upon him that he cried, "You infernal devil,
if—"

Realization of his helplessness stopped his mouth. He waited.
A great hand thrust out and the strong fingers twisted into his
hair, which he wore quite long. Looking up, quite fascinated by
the horror, it seemed to him that the red-gray beard barely
sufficed to cover a grin of pleasant anticipation. Then the white-
hot iron was thrust against his forehead.

He closed his eyes. A hot fume and smoke of burning flesh
choked him. He felt the burning point pass down his forehead.
Then it crossed the first mark with a line to the side.

CHAPTER V

THE LONGEST days are our silent days of inaction. And the weeks which followed were to Jack Bristol a more interminable period than all the life which went before. He was guarded night and day with the most scrupulous care, and when his captor, whose name he had discovered in the interim to be "Hank" Sherry, left the cabin to go hunting, Jack was chained like a dog in the corner, and hands and feet secured so that he could not stir. For the rest, when Hank was at home he allowed his captive a reasonable liberty.

Twice a day, immediately after the branding of Jack's forehead, the mountaineer had changed the dressing upon the wound, treating it with the utmost care. But as for the reason behind the mutilation, or as for the purpose for which Jack was held in the shack, no information was vouchsafed. On any other subject Hank Sherry was voluble. Though he chiefly dwelt upon the exploits and prowess of Charlie, the last of his sons, yet he was quite willing to talk of other things, such as hunting, or storm and stress of weather there in the mountains, or any of a thousand topics, saving any which tended to expose his past life. And so the long days passed slowly, one into another, until a time came when big Hank Sherry sat opposite him at the supper table, combing his red-gray beard and staring out of his red-fringed eyes.

"Suppose a man wants to get a dog fighting mad, what does he do with him?" asked the mountaineer. He went on to answer his own question, turning his face away from Jack in that way he had, and addressing his speech to a distant corner. "He takes the dog and ties him up and waits till he gets will to be free. Then he sets him loose. And the hardest job he has is to get himself out of the way of that dog's teeth."

The glance of Hank reverted for an instant to Jack.

"Suppose I was to turn you loose?"

Jack looked hastily down, but even so the other had seen the sudden and fierce light of exultation.

"What you're thinking," said Hank, "is that you'd jump for my throat and work your hands through my beard till you got a grip on the windpipe."

Still looking to the corner, he slipped his own hand under his beard and seemed to touch his throat tenderly.

"But if I was to say to you first, 'Give me your word of honor that if I turn you free you'll not lay a hand on me,' what would you say?"

Jack Bristol made no answer. But he watched the big man as a fox watches the chicken beyond the shielding net of wire. Hank laughed softly. There was something about the attitude of the other which seemed to please him immensely.

"Blood," said he, "that's what you want. Oh, I can see that! I see a bull terrier go at a Great Dane, once. He slipped in under him and set his teeth in the Dane's throat. There was a lot of threshing around, but in the finish the Dane lay down on his side nice and peaceable and the terrier choked him to death. And if you got at me, it'd be the same story."

He shook his head, his eyes looking afar upon the remembered battle. He seemed more pleased than ever.

"The fine part of it," continued Hank, "is that you're going to be on my side agin the rest of 'em, in the end."

"On your side?" said Jack Bristol.

"I'm a patient man," said Hank. "I'm willing to wait and wait. And now about that promise. Most like you been telling yourself over and over what you're going to do when the time comes that you get loose. You been seeing my eyes get glassy in your dreams. That's why I got to have your promise. You hear?"

Jack paused. If mere words could buy his freedom, would he not be pardoned if he broke his vow when his hands were loosed?

"What promise?" he asked.

"Why, a promise that you'll do me no harm."

"I'll give you that, then."

Hank nodded and behind the vast shrubbery of his beard he seemed to be smiling.

"Keep right on thinking," he said. "You keep it in your head that if I wanted to play safe I could dig another hole out yonder. I could make it big enough to hold a hoss and a man. And after I put you and your Susan hoss in it, who'd ever guess that you'd been here? Who'd ever ask questions?"

The skin prickled upon Jack's head.

"You can't keep murder under your hat," he declared. "It comes out sooner or later."

"How many has been up to ask about Charlie?" remarked the mountaineer. "Been some weeks now, and there ain't been a soul by to speak for him, has there?"

Into the silence drifted the cry of a wolf, howling on the verge of mute distance. In some way it showed Jack more plainly than words could have done, how utterly he was in the hands of the other.

"I've given you my word," he said.

"And you've had a chance to think it over," said the mountaineer, "so there you are!"

As he spoke, he took from the table the razor-edge butcher knife. He took no time to untie ropes which he would not need again. One slash set the feet of Jack at liberty. Another cut free the hands which had been tied behind his back. He was loosed from his bonds! His life was set suddenly to music of a higher scale. His strength of body was multiplied. And in the grip of his hands stood the man who had brutally disfigured him for life and then chained him up like a dog. He crouched that infinitesimal bit which tells of tensed muscles ready to leap and strike.

But big Hank Sherry had calmly turned his back, tossed the butcher knife onto the table, and now approached the stove, lifted a lid, and shoved in a stick of wood to replenish the dying fire. As he did this, he was engaged in humming faintly an old tune whose words Jack had never known, but whose music he could never forget thereafter. His own fury to attack was checked and dammed up in him. He could not spring at the man while his back was turned.

The fire was roaring again around the new fuel. Hank replaced the lid and turned—not directly toward Jack, but merely enough so that the latter could see the face of his late captor covered with sudden perspiration. So he walked straight toward the door of the cabin.

"Sherry!" called Jack.

The latter halted, seemed about to turn, and Jack set himself to rush while, in a semi-hysterical fury, he felt possessed of strength enough to tear the big man limb from limb. But after that momentary halt, the mountaineer continued straight on his way and went out into the night. Still, for an instant, Jack stared at the door. Then he rushed out into the night, but he found that the other had melted away among the trees near his house.

"Sherry!" he called at the top of his voice. "Sherry! Where are you?"

He heard no answer and at length he turned and stamped back into the cabin. As his disappointment subsided, he was beginning to realize the consummate nerve and steadiness which the older man had shown. He had known that the plighted word of his captive meant little or nothing in such an extremity. But he had trusted to the instinctive honor which would keep the man of the desert from attacking while his back was turned.

At least, the mountaineer would return after he had allowed his late captive sufficient time to cool down. To fill that interval there was one thing of importance for Jack to do.

In the corner was the old closet in which Sherry had placed the mirror on the first day. Jack took the ax which leaned against the wall and with one stroke smashed the lock. Then from the interior of the closet he saw the faint glimmer of glass as the lantern played feebly upon it. He snatched the mirror out, held it up, and looked upon the image of his face for the first time since his captivity began.

What he saw was a black and curling beard that covered the lower part of his face. All the skin that the beard did not cover was extraordinarily pale. But whiter by far than the skin of his forehead was a scar which formed a perfect cross, glistening in his flesh. Truly he was branded forever!

With a cry he snatched up the revolver from the holster of the mountaineer hanging against the wall, and with that weapon in his hand, he ran out into the night. In a blind madness he ranged among the trees. Twice he fired into empty shadows which seemed to move.

And so he came back at last to the cabin and saw, by the lantern light, the peaceful figure of the mountaineer with his stool tilted back against the wall while he whittled calmly at a piece of wood and puffed on his pipe. "Stand up!" thundered Jack.

But Hank Sherry merely removed the pipe from his teeth and shook his head as though in gentle reproof.

"It looks to me," he said, "like the end of a day's work. Why should I stand up?"

"Because it's the end of a life and a day all at the same minute," said Jack. "Damn you, get up!"

"I've got your word," replied the other.

"You yaller livered skunk!" cried Jack. "D'you dare to talk about promises to me? You tried to murder me sleeping. Now you talk about honor?"

"My honor?" echoed the big man, and as always his voice remained singularly small and even. "I ain't said a word about my honor. What I'm talking about is yours. Lord God, man, I've done pretty near every bad thing in the calendar; and I've busted more'n one promise amongst the rest. But ain't you different? Why, sure you are. If I hadn't knowed you was different, d'you think I'd of trusted to your promise? I knowed that you'd get heated up at first, and that's why I kept my back to you. But after a while I come back because I figured that when I seen you, there'd be no more'n a lot of words and smoke and no fire. And I see that I'm right! You're talking hard, partner, but you ain't got it in you to do what you think you can do!"

Jack dropped onto a nearby stool. The revolver clattered upon the floor. He buried his face in his hands. As the thoughts whirled maddeningly through his brain he realized that Hank Sherry was right, and still that steady voice went on.

"Ten minutes is all you needed. And if you come right down to it, ten minutes is all most folks need. The things we do that send us to hell, and the things we do that send us the other way—why, there's only ten minutes thinking between 'em!"

CHAPTER VI

H E WAITED not even to shave the black beard from his face, but in five minutes his pack was made and he was on the back of brown Susan. From the darkness beside him he heard the mountaineer calling, "So long! I'll be seeing you later, son!"

Jack returned no answer. The very sound of Sherry's voice roused him to a wild desire for murder. But in another moment Susan was at full gallop across the clearing and the fresh wind was beating into his face, and blowing out of his memory all the horrors of the cabin.

That shuddering sense that he was marked to the end of time kept him cold of heart as the good mare climbed the first long grade toward the west, but, after a time that thought began to grow smaller and smaller in his mind. And finally it was forgotten.

For he was young, and the night was new, and over his shoulder he could look at the pale, thin sickle of a new moon rising, and no matter through what horrors he had passed, the point of importance was that they now lay behind him.

He climbed the top of that long slope. Below him, he saw a valley opening out, long and narrow among the peaks, and brown Susan went down the descent like a racing deer. Before she reached the leveler going below, Jack Bristol was on the verge of singing, and all that had happened fifteen miles behind him among the mountains might as well have been fifteen years ago.

It was a pleasant valley into which he had dropped out of the highlands. It was thick with houses. A narrow river went talking through the midst of it, and it watered a fertile land on either side. For the fields were small, telling of close tillage. The barns were numerous, which told that the yield was rich.

He could not make out much in details, for now a mist of high-blown clouds began to veil even the faint light of the new moon; but he could at least make out the forms of horses and cattle in the pastures. And even in the dark of night he could sense the happy prosperity of that region.

Brown Susan, in the meantime, was frolicking along a road far smoother and better kept than those to which she was accustomed. And she made the best of the fast going. She had a colt's love of sprinting, and now she kept up on the bit, fairly dancing with an eagerness to get away. Once or twice Jack indulged her, but on the whole he kept her back to a steady jog. He had only one great purpose in mind, and that was to put as much distance as possible between himself and the cabin among the mountains. At one long ride he wanted to get out of the district of all who might know Hank Sherry and his branded forehead.

A schoolhouse, aflare with lights for some entertainment or dance, sadly shook his purpose, however. It was many a long week since he had danced, and now the sound of a shrill violin, blowing faintly to him, made Jack Bristol turn Susan to the side and bring her up into the shadow of a dense little grove of trees.

From this point of vantage he could hear every strain of the music, and even the slipping of dancing feet upon the floor was plainly audible. Between dances, too, he saw the couples pour out of the little school and waltz hither and yon over the schoolyard, and then their voices, and even fragments of their talk floated plainly to him. It was all wonderfully enticing to Jack.

The deep voices of the men were like a challenge; the sweet voices of the girls were like a call to him. In another time he would have ridden to the hitching racks and tethered his horse and gone in to find a partner, but now he carried on his forehead the brand which held him more effectually than even rope or chain could have done. For the first time there dawned in his brain an understanding of what Sherry might have meant when he said that he would soon see Jack again. For might not the world shun him and drive him back to the one shelter which remained open to him?

That thought had hardly come home to him with a stunning blow when he heard two voices, speaking so close to him that they seemed to blow up out of the ground.

"—so I said, 'Let 'er stop, then. Cut me off. I'll get on by myself.'"

"Lee, why are you always so antagonistic when you talk with your father?"

"Because he's always so antagonistic when he talks with me."

"But he has a right to talk severely to his own son."

"Not about you, Nell. He can damn me all he pleases about other things, but when he begins to talk about you—"

The man paused in a silence of outraged and virtuous indignation. For a moment the girl did not answer.

"Just what does he say?" asked Nell at length.

"In the first place, he strings out a long lingo about what I owe to my family."

"Don't laugh at that, Lee. It is an old family and it has an honorable record."

"There'll be nothing in the whole record as fine as my marriage with Nell Carney."

"You silly boy!" breathed Nell. And her pleasure put a quiver in her voice. "You'll never listen to reason."

"After we're married, then I'll listen to tons of reason."

"But has he anything else against me? Dad's poverty, I suppose."

"No, that doesn't bother the governor. But he has an idea that I should be making a good fat income before I marry. That's nonsense! Mining engineers don't begin on a salary equal to a millionaire's income. I tell him that, but he refuses to see the light! But once we marry, Nell, we'll—"

"Do you really think that might change him?"

"Think? I know! It couldn't help but change him!"

"Oh, listen!"

The music struck into a swinging waltz.

"Well, what's up?" queried the man.

"Don't you hear? Let's hurry in!"

"That waltz? I danced to that last winter till I was sick of it. No, let's stay here. There's something more important than dancing, I guess!"

She was silent. Then Jack could hear her humming the air lightly. Her escort, in the meantime, lighted a match and applied it to a "tailor-made" cigarette. The flare showed Jack Bristol, first of all, a big, well-made, handsome youth in his middle twenties, nattily dressed, with his hair sleek back on his head. Then, as the cigarette caught the flame and he opened his cupped hands, the smoker allowed the light to reach to the girl opposite him. It was only for a flash before the match streaked downward to the ground and was tramped out. But in the first flash Bristol saw enough.

From that instant what they said on the far side of the tree was not simply casual chatter. Every word she uttered was of vital importance that tugged Jack forward in his saddle and held him breathless to the end, as though she were disposing of his destiny as well as her own.

"Now, to get down to business," said the man of the tailor-made cigarette, "I'll tell you what I really think—that when you marry me the old man will rave like the devil for a few days, and after that he'll forgive us and take us home!"

"Take us home?" echoed the girl a little sharply. "But I don't want to be taken home. I don't want to sit about in that big house of your father's and have your family circle about in the offing freezing me with glances and half-smiles!"

"They'll never do that, dear. Ten minutes of you in that house will thaw out the whole crew. They'll forget themselves and fall in love with you in a flock. I know them, Nell!"

"But after all, don't you want to start a home of your own, Lee?"

"That used to be the idea," said the man, "but times have changed. This is the twentieth century and homes don't start without plenty of coin mixed in with the foundation concrete. Don't be out of date, my dear!"

"You say that in a rather patronizing way," protested the girl with a touch of acid in her tone that pleased Jack immensely.

"I don't mean it in that way," answered the other at once. "But the point, Nell, is that we have use for the old man even if he has no use for us!" He laughed at his joke. Jack noticed that he laughed alone. "A man can't get along on a beggarly beginner's salary," went on Lee. "Not when he's been raised as I've been raised. It won't do. A man can't bring up his son to million dollar tastes and then dodge him, all at once, and tell him to start for himself. And the old man wouldn't dream of doing that—not if I'd marry where he wants me to marry. Don't you see how the whole nasty mess turns out? First he gives me the tastes of an English lord, and when those tastes are fixed in my blood he has me in his power. He can dictate my course of action. If I displease him, no matter where or when, he can simply hold over my head the threat of cutting off my allowance—"

"Lee! You don't mean to say that you still get an allowance from him!"

"Why not, dear? Why not? Anything disgraceful in that? Good gad, they pay mining engineers nothing to speak of but experience for the first few years. And a man can't keep up his bridge, to say nothing of his poker, when his salary is chiefly experience."

He laughed again at this jest, and again he laughed alone. Once more Jack was greatly pleased.

"The thing for us to do," declared Lee at length, "is to step out and get married and tell the old man about it later. That's what I've fixed up for tonight."

"Lee! I didn't tell you—"

"I didn't have time to ask you first. I knew you'd agree."

"But I don't agree!"

"You will when I explain. You see, it was devilish hard for me to break away this evening. It has taken three days of lies for me to lay all the plans. And even now, if I go back, I'll have to face a battery of questions. So I decided that we'd make the fullest possible use of our time and that will be to ride down the road and let the minister—"

"Lee, what on earth are you talking about?"

There was a breath of silence, then, "Nell, have I taken too much for granted? Haven't you really meant what you said to me? Or was it as I've often suspected simply that when they carried me into your house all smashed up by the fall from that fool of a horse, you set your teeth and decided that you'd save my life simply because it was so nearly gone; and when my life was saved you thought that you were in love with me simply because you'd been with me so long! Is that it?"

Jack Bristol liked the stranger better than before. He had spoken slowly, seriously, humbly.

"No," said the girl. "It isn't that. I really do care for you, Lee. But a marriage like that—"

"What's wrong with it? You're as hot-headed as they come. I know you don't object to the rush of it, Nell!"

"No, not a bit. Not if it was serious and honest. But it isn't. It's all a bluff with which we're trying to force your father's hand. Isn't that so?"

"A bluff? No, it's a great big game, Nell!"

"That's a polite name for it!"

"Will you do one thing?"

"Of course."

"Then get your horse and ride down the road. I'll meet you there in ten minutes beyond the cemetery. We can have it out on the road. If you don't agree—well, it will have to stand that way. If you do agree, then we'll be on the way to the minister's house. Is that fair, Nell?"

"I suppose so, but—"

"You've given your word!" cried Lee eagerly.

"Very well, then," said the girl without enthusiasm. "I'll be there!"

CHAPTER VII

JACK WATCHED them go. He waited until they were well out of sight toward the schoolhouse and the tangle of horses in front of the building. Then he drew back brown Susan and surveyed the road.

He had no right to come any further into the business than his involuntary eavesdropping had, in the first place, brought him. But he had no full control over what he did that evening.

The long imprisonment in the Sherry cabin among the upper mountains had served to store up an immense energy in him. Now it was striving for an outlet, and the first opportunity which he saw was to work with might and main to prevent the meeting of the young mining engineer and the girl.

What he should do after that did not enter his head. The first and important task was to see that the two did not meet again.

Now he saw the girl go scurrying down the road on a fast-stepping galloper. She disappeared around a distant bend, and after a considerable interval, another figure on horseback followed, a big man on a big horse. Unquestionably it must be the man named Lee.

Jack let him go back. Then he loosed brown Susan in pursuit. She had traveled hard and far already this night, but the brief rest under the trees had been sufficient to breathe her. Once more she was full of running, and she showed her delight on being turned loose by sprinting down the road at a dizzy pace that brought her in striking distance of the other within the first half mile. Indeed, so swift was her approach that though the velvet dust on the road muffled her hoofbeats, the big man turned in his saddle to watch his pursuer.

"Hello!" called Jack Bristol.

And as he waved his hand in the dark, the other drew rein and waved in return. Jack swept up on him like a thunderbolt. It was hardly fair, but he had been lately deeply schooled in unfair tactics.

"What's up?" called the other.

"A fight, damn you!" said Jack, and as the mare shot alongside, he leaned, wound his arms around the waist of Lee, and dragged him out of the saddle while Susan went by.

As for the gray which Lee had been riding, no sooner did it feel the weight lifting from reins and saddle than it flirted heels high in the air and then bolted down a by-path and across country.

"Hell and fire!" shouted the dismounted man. "Is this a joke or a hold-up? You infernal hound, I'll break you in two!"

He had twisted around as he spoke. In vain Jack strove to free himself from his burden. In another instant they both toppled heavily to the ground while brown Susan danced a few paces away and stood watching them, deeply bewildered, with one ear pricked and one ear back. Surely it was strange to see men act as these were acting.

Taken by surprise in the first onset, the mining engineer needed only an instant to rouse himself, and then he proved a man's task to handle. For he had some twenty odd pounds of advantage in weight, and all that advantage was in trained muscle. Besides, he was a skilled boxer and wrestler. Jack could tell that in an instant, for as they fell he found himself caught in a bone-crushing grip that threatened to smash in his ribs. He freed himself from that hold by clipping his fist across the back of Lee's head. With an oath the latter disentangled himself and sprang to his feet.

Up himself with the speed of a cat, Jack was in time to duck under a straight-shooting left. And then he began to fight!

He began to fight with a silent song somewhere behind his lips. He began to fight as he had not fought since he was a child. For in latter years in moments of crises it had been gunplay, always, and never fists. But a good lesson once learned can never be entirely forgotten. The old rhythm of dancing feet and darting hands returned to him almost at once. And he put into the fury of his attack all of the unspent wrath which had been heaping up in him since Hank Sherry caught and made him a prisoner.

Big Lee, trained athlete and courageous man that he was, fought back heartily, but Jack split upon him as rain splits upon a roof-rim. It was in vain that Lee stopped one rush with a thudding blow which landed squarely on Jack's chest. It was in vain that he knocked the smaller man flying with a second pile-driver which snapped flush upon the point of his chin. For Jack rebounded from the earth and dove in again for more. His left hand was a shadow with a weight of a sledgehammer flying in it; his right hand was a thrust of flameless fire. Before the one, big Lee staggered; and when the right crashed home he went down on his face, wrapped in a heavy sleep.

Jack Bristol, singing through his teeth, dropped to his knees and pressed an ear to the back of the fallen man. The beat of the heart was slow but steady. And Jack sprang up again, leaped into the saddle upon Susan, and sent her off down the road again at a rattling pace.

In his heart, too, there was a sense of great and satisfactory accomplishment. The waters of wrath which had been piling up in him for the many days had now burst the dam and were expended. In his heart, there was only a great goodwill toward all the world.

He put a mile and a half behind him. Then, to the left, he saw the pale glimmer of the white headstones in the graveyard, seen indistinctly through the night and among the trunks of the trees which overgrew the cemetery. He rounded the curve beyond it, and there was the girl, her horse only faintly perceptible where it stood beneath a thin screen of young poplars.

But Jack reined Susan to a stop nearby.

"Lady," he called, "I'm bringing you a message."

She rode out to meet him.

"A message?" she echoed him. "From whom? And who are you?"

"From Lee."

"And?" she urged.

"He can't come."

"Ah!"

"There was an accident."

"Of what nature?" asked the girl.

"He met a man, and—"

"Well?"

"And there was trouble."

"About what? Good heavens, what are you trying to say? Has Lee been hurt? I heard no gun!" cried the girl, and the dread and pain in her voice went through and through Jack. "One of those brutal bullies—some gun-fighter who hated him for his good English and his clothes. Oh, tell me everything—no—I can find out what has happened when—take your hand off my reins!"

For as she started to spur past him, Jack caught at the reins and stopped her.

"There's no such hurry," said he. "He ain't hurt bad. There was no gunplay."

"But you said there was trouble—"

"There was. It was all with the hands, though, that trouble."

"They mobbed him, then!" cried the girl in angry scorn. "Oh, the cowards."

"Maybe you'd call it a mob," said Jack, and he grinned in spite of himself, "but there was only one man that stopped him."

"One man!" breathed the girl. "One man stopped Lee Jarvis? I don't believe it!"

"He'll be coming along in ten or fifteen minutes," said Jack. "Then you can ask him. He's got to catch his hoss first, and after that he'll be coming along."

"But he sent you—? I don't understand. My head is whirling. Will you tell me just what happened?"

"It all started," said Jack, "when he scratched a match."

"Is this a joke?"

"Not for me, lady. I'm plumb serious."

"Then try to explain, if you please."

"You're willing to wait here till Lee comes along?"

"Of course; that is, if he hasn't been seriously hurt."

"It goes back to that match I was talking about," said Jack. "When he lighted that match and his cigarette he thought that as the end—"

"Ah," cried the girl, "I think I understand! You were under those trees! You were eavesdropping!"

"I was just listening in," said Jack, "because I thought it would save you and him from a pile of embarrassment, at first, if I didn't tell you that I was there and that somebody else had heard the secret. It didn't make no difference what I heard because I was on my way West and out of this part of the country, and I'd never see you or hear of you again. You see that?"

"I don't fully understand anything you say."

"But then he scratched that match," said Jack, "and—d'you know what an old man I once knew used to say? That a pretty girl belonged to the whole wide world; every man jack of us had a right to admire 'em! But that's what the match showed me."

"What in the world is in your mind?" cried the girl, and now her voice was a trifle high and strained.

"Well," said Jack, "when I saw your face I knew that it wouldn't work."

"You knew what?"

"I knew that Jarvis could never put his deal through because you'd never help him, and you'd never help him because it wasn't square!"

He paused. The girl did not reply.

"But at the same time, there was no use letting him try to sweep you off your feet," went on Jack. "So, after you'd gone by, I waited until I saw him start up the road, and then I dropped in behind and stopped him. We had a little argument, and he stayed behind, and here I am!"

"Will you let me pass?" asked the girl in a very small voice. "Will you let me go back?"

"I see," nodded Jack. "You're afraid. But, after all, I guess you won't go."

So saying, he dropped the reins and drew Susan back. She stepped away nimbly and allowed plenty of room to the girl to ride down the road. In fact, she spoke to her horse, but she drew the animal up before it could make a step. One prophecy, at least, had come true!

CHAPTER VIII

ONCE MORE they faced each other in a breathing space of silence, and how eloquent, felt Jack Bristol, silence could be.

"Why did you say that?" asked the girl at length.

"That you wouldn't ride away yet?"

"Yes. What made you presume to read my mind like that?"

"Because," said Jack, "I'd seen your face by the light of that match."

"You talk queer nonsense," said the girl.

"And I knew," continued Jack, "that you wouldn't run where there was no danger."

"I wonder," said the girl, "if you are not more dangerous than you seem. But will you continue and tell me everything?"

"Why I stopped him?"

"It makes my blood boil to think that any one man could stop him," cried the girl.

"It was a lucky right," said Jack meditatively.

"A what?"

"It landed right on the point of the chin," said Jack. "He went to sleep as though someone were rocking a cradle."

"Ah," said the girl, "no matter by what trickery you struck him down—"

She paused.

"To go right back to the beginning," said Jack, "I saw that it wouldn't be right for you to meet him. Because it wouldn't be square."

"Not honest?"

"Not exactly. What Jarvis wants to do is to hold up the old man by marrying you. He figures that his father ain't going to let his son live too poor. So he'll take a chance on marrying you and waiting for old Jarvis to raise the coin. Isn't that the straight of it?"

"It's—but why should I talk about such things with you?"

"Because it's night," said Jack, "and it don't do no harm to let a gent that you'll never see again help you think."

"And I'm never to see you again?" asked the girl, taking up that part of his statement.

"Never," said Jack. "I'm gone before morning if there's any luck with me."

"Who are you?"

"I can't tell you that. If I could be so free with my name I wouldn't be in such a hurry."

"You've done something wrong," said the girl eagerly, "and you're running away from the consequences?"

"I've done something right," corrected Jack, "by keeping a girl from doing something wrong."

"You've chosen to act as my conscience, then?"

"I've done what ten minutes of thinking would have made you do," said Jack. He quoted old Sherry with gusto. "I stepped in between you and a jump in the dark, that's all."

"What makes you so sure?"

"Because if you'd have waited for him here, you'd have gone on with him."

"Never! That is—not unless I'd made up my mind that he was right."

"That's what you think you'd have done. But I figure that you couldn't help yourself. Once folks get started—why, it's like trying to dam a river that's running down a steep hill. They climb right over the dam. Nope, you couldn't help yourself, lady. Besides, it's at night. And when folks can't see what's around 'em all chances look good. It's what the night does. Suppose you'd met me like this by daylight. D'you think I'd of had a chance to talk one minute to you? Nope, you'd of rode on down the trail and showed me nothing but a cloud of dust."

"You're a very queer fellow," said the girl. "And I think you're right about part of what you say. How do you explain it? Why am I staying here and listening?"

"Because it's the faces of people that we're afraid of; not their talk. It isn't what they say. It's the ugly faces of 'em while they're saying it. Am I right?"

"I suppose you are," said the girl slowly. "And—"

"Listen!" broke in Jack.

Down the road came the rapid and muffled beat of the hoofs of a horse.

"It's Lee Jarvis coming on the jump to get you," said Jack.

"Oh!" cried the girl.

"We can hide by riding down that alley," said Jack.

"Hide? Why should I hide?"

"Do I have to fight him again?"

"Fight?"

"Lady," said Jack, "it's been a long time since I've had a real, honest-Injun, all-leather fight. If you say the word him and me tangle. But if you figure there's a premium on his face, just ride down that little trail with me and wait under the trees till he's tired of looking for you around here."

"This outrage—" cried the girl.

"There's no time for talk," said Jack. "You can lay to this, lady: I ain't started all the trouble that I've taken tonight to give up at the last minute without a fight. You can tell me what you think of me and my kind later on!"

There was a muffled exclamation from the girl. Then, without a word, she swung the head of her horse to one side and galloped him down the lane. It was but a twisting little bridle path among the trees and instantly they were lost to view from the main road. A hundred yards from their starting place, Jack dropped from the saddle and, standing in front of the girl's horse, held his hand ready to choke off a neigh if Jarvis' horse should be heard in the distance. At the same time he spoke to Susan, and the mare came up and nosed his shoulder inquisitively.

In the meantime, the beat of the hoofs of the Jarvis horse sounded small and dull on the road. The sound stopped. There was silence for a minute or two. Then the hoofbeats were heard retreating.

"And there you are," said Jack, swinging back into the saddle once more. "The thing's done and no bones broken."

Her answer astonished him.

"You and your horse are wonderful chums," she said. "It's easy to see that."

"Susan and I?" said Jack, gaping at the girl through the darkness. "Of course we are, but, lady, suppose I see you home?"

She began to laugh, and the sound of that laughter paralyzed Jack. At a stroke, the initiative, which he had maintained from the first, was lost to him.

"I can find my way home alone," said this strange girl, who seemed to rise all the stronger out of defeat. "But if you wish to come along, why, I'll be very glad to have you."

He fell in at her side. They cut straight across country, jumping the fences as they came to each barrier. They went at first in another of the silences which, from time to time, fell between them. But after a time she said, "Of course, you were wrong about one thing, and that was that I could be swept off my feet by Lee Jarvis."

"Maybe I was wrong," said Jack humbly. "Right now I'd figure that you could handle about anything."

"That's a way men have," said the girl. "After they've done something for a woman—"

She stopped herself short and switched to a new topic.

"A little while ago you said that you were never coming into this part of the country again. I really wish that you'd tell me why."

"When I started through," said Jack slowly, "it was because I wanted to get out to new country. But now there's another main reason."

"Well?"

"It's one I can't tell you."

"That's not fair," said the girl. "You know I'll never rest until I hear what it is."

"I couldn't tell you," said Jack frankly, "except that I'm never to see you again; but you're the reason, lady. If you were a little bit different, I'd come back through hell-fire to find you again. But if I talked to you long enough you'd do nothing but laugh at my grammar."

She shook her head.

"I think it would take a most unusual person to laugh at you on any account," she said. "And certainly bad grammar is nothing but—"

She came to another abrupt pause, reining in her horse.

"There's my house, d'you see? That's dad's house yonder on top of that little hill."

"I'll stop here, then."

"You won't take me to my door?"

"If you want me to," said Jack sadly, and not another word passed between them until he had reached the horse shed and drawn the saddle from her horse.

"I wonder if Lee Jarvis has come here already to inquire about me?" murmured the girl.

"I figure he won't," answered Jack. "He doesn't bother your father much, eh?"

He was walking by her side toward the house, with brown Susan following at his heels. Now the girl stopped short.

"Why did you say that? How did you know that? And who *can* you be?"

"Lady," said Jack. "I'm a friend that wishes you luck. Let it go at that."

She walked on. Before he knew it they stood at the door of the house.

"Good-by," said Jack, and held out his hand. "Good-by, and good luck, and no Lee Jarvis in your luck!"

Instead of taking the extended hand, she struck back sharply at the door which flew wide and allowed a bright shaft of light to fall upon Jack. He saw the half-mischievous smile of expectation which had formed upon her lips die. Her eyes, fixed on his face, grew large with terror, and with a shriek she turned and fled into the house—fled in mortal agony of terror, with her head half turned to watch the horror pursue.

And Jack knew that she had seen the cross on his forehead.

CHAPTER IX

I F THERE were men about the place that woman's scream
would bring them out with guns in their hands. Jack Bristol
paused to ask no questions. He flung himself back into the
saddle on the mare and put her over the first fence and then
cantered across the meadow beyond. In the meantime, the little
house behind him, which he had been watching over his shoulder, fairly boiled with life. Lights stirred across the windows.
Three or four men ran out, slamming doors and shouting to
one another. A lantern went swinging toward the barn. Then
someone sighted the fugitive. There was no preliminary warning,
no call to him to stop, but a rifle began crackling at once in the
hands of an expert, for only an expert, shooting at such a distant
and moving target by such a light could have put his bullets so
close to the mark.

A word to Susan sent her on a re-doubled speed and out of
all danger almost at once. But as she leaped the fence into the
open road, Jack heard the quick rattling of hoofbeats across a
wooden culvert far behind and knew that the armed men of
that household were out upon his trail, and out for blood.

Not until this moment did he have an opportunity to think,
but he could come to no conclusion. All that he knew was that
the girl had seen the gleaming scar on his forehead and after
that she had fled with a shriek, as though from a wild beast!
But what did that cross represent? Why had it been placed
upon the faces of Hank Sherry and his son Charlie? Who had

placed it there? A horrible explanation began to form dimly in the back of his brain, but before it became a real conclusion, the remembered shriek of the girl ran back across his mind and blotted out the rest.

In the meantime, they could never catch brown Susan. The run from the upper mountains had, apparently, merely served to loosen her muscles. The pause while the master talked to the girl had completely rested the mare again, and now she was as full of running as ever.

So Jack let her drop back until the pursuers were fairly close. The wind had scoured the sky clean of all clouds, by this time. And in the faint light of the sickle moon he saw the blotchy shapes of the riders bobbing up and down as they spurred in pursuit. Now and again they loosed a scattered volley at him in the chance of striking the man or the horse with a random shot, but all those bullets flew wild, and Jack laughed at their efforts. He would win one small revenge out of this night's work, he decided. He would lead them at his heels until dawn, making them think, every moment, that they were about to run him down. And at the end of that time, he would simply canter away from them as though on the wings of the wind.

Indeed, the horses behind were laboring at full speed, while Susan, keeping up her long, striding gallop, was holding them even without an effort. Two miles, three miles flew beneath her, and Jack was forced to rein her in as the pace told on the riders behind. He saw a fork in the road before him, now, and was about to take the branch to the left, because it promised to lead out of the valley and into the higher ground beyond, when he saw, by the growing moonlight, a sweep of a dozen horsemen coming far off down that road. With an oath he swung Susan onto the other road.

But how had they been able to spread the alarm? He looked up, and he saw the moonlight running in a cluster of straight, horizontal lines above him. Telephone wires, of course; what a consummate fool he had been! He had thought to play tag with them and they, in the meantime, were throwing a circle of danger around him. While the men rode at his heels, the girl stayed at the telephone spreading the alarm. Jack Bristol looked away at the tall mountains to the left from which he had been shut off, then he loosed the reins and Susan bounded away.

But a wild yelling began the instant he turned onto that right fork. And the yelling was echoed from squarely in front of him. Yes, down the road before him swung a new body of horsemen, small with distance, but riding hard. They had blocked him on every road.

But he turned Susan to the right and sent her sailing over the fence into the open field beyond. What difference did it make to her whether she ran on smooth roads or rough fields? She flew like a swallow, dipping up and down with her long leaps, and crossed the wide field, sailed the next fence, again, and—struck in new-ploughed ground beyond!

Jack, with an exclamation of dismay, felt her flounder into a laboring trot through the muck, and leaning to the side, he peered ahead to make out how far the field extended. The moon-haze was thick before him, but in the little distance he could make out the outlines of a fence. Toward this, then, he pressed on, and glancing back over his shoulder he saw the posses tearing across the field in pursuit and gaining now at a fearful rate.

Well, let them run as they pleased. When they reached the ploughed ground it would stop them more effectually than a wall of stone. Brown Susan, stepping more than fetlock deep, struggled on toward the fence, stepped onto a strip of firmer going just beside it, leaped the obstacle like a cat, and landed on deeper and newer ploughed ground just beyond!

That was the meaning, then, of the triumphant shouting behind him and to the sides. They understood that he had run into a trap from which there was no exit. No, he was helpless, for looking to the side, he saw a group of riders spurring down some undiscovered lane to skirt around and gain the front of him. There, hemmed in on all sides, they would shoot him to death from a safe distance.

Already they were opening fire. The rifle bullets began to sing their short, weird lyrics in his ears. Another moment and gallant Sue would be struck. So Jack sprang to the top of the fence, so that his body would be clearly outlined, and threw up his hands. The firing ceased almost at once. Men began to run across the ploughed area toward him, and Susan, knowing well enough that they had been in flight from just those people, crowded close and whinneyed softly and anxiously to call him away.

They came around him with a rush. They came silently, like wolves that are wild with starvation. And literally they leaped at his throat. Men sprang from either side. He was smashed to the ground. His revolver was torn from him. His arms were bound behind his back. Then he was dragged to his feet again.

He found a crowd of more than thirty angry faces around him, all dimly and ominously outlined in the moonlight. Out of the jargon of many fierce voices speaking at the same time came a call for silence.

"It's Captain Carney," said some of those nearest. "Let's hear what he has to say."

"We'll get a light, first," said the heavy voice which had been calling for silence. "We'll get a light and see that Nell wasn't looking at a ghost that didn't exist. Girls are tolerable skittish and they see double when they get excited. But if it should turn out to be what she said, we ain't going to act hasty, boys, are we?"

"We'll talk it over plumb quiet, Cap," answered the other.

So Captain Carney scratched a match whose first light showed Jack the face of a middle-aged man, a stern face but the face of a just man, withal. Next that light was cupped in the shielding hands of the captain, and when the flame had flared out to the full the hands opened and a yellow burst of light fell on Jack. It brought a shout from the crowd.

"It's him! I seen it clear as day! There's an oak, yonder, and I got a rope that ain't working. Let's finish him right here and now, Cap!"

Men from the rear began crowding in. Hands reached for Jack, but the father of Nell struck those hands away.

"Boys," he said, "you ain't here to butcher a maverick. This here is a man the same as you and me—"

"That's wrong as hell," thundered someone. "He's a coyote done up in a man's hide!"

That exclamation brought a growl from the others.

"That's a true word. No use wasting words over him, Cap! Shoot the dog and leave him lie!"

Jack twisted himself away from restraining hands. He pressed close to Carney.

"Captain!" he shouted through the rising clamor, "for God's sake give me half a chance. I'm not the man you think. Let me have five minutes to prove it!"

Captain Carney dropped a reassuring hand upon his shoulder.

"You're going to have a chance to talk," he said. "Don't worry about that. Boys, stand off, will you? Give him a chance to say what he's got to say. Give him five minutes, boys!"

His huge voice cleared a circle. The others pressed back and waited.

"Now speak up, Sherry," said Captain Carney. "Boil it down and make your yarn short, and leave out all the lies you can. We know that you're talking for your life and that may make you want to string out the story. But make it short or we'll have to interrupt you, and if we interrupt you there won't be no chance of you speaking again!"

"Boys," said Jack. "I'll tell you the straight of things just the way they happened. I was coming over the mountains a few weeks back and I hit on a house in the evening just when it begun to get dark. Seemed nacheral to ask for chuck and a place to sleep here. I done just that and a gent with a hook nose and

reddish looking eyes let me in. That night while I was asleep
they decided to murder me, but when they tackled me I managed
to fight back. I killed Hank Sherry's son, Charlie, with his own
gun, but then Hank knocked me out.

"He knocked me stiff, tied me up, and then heated a poker
red-hot and burned this cross into my forehead. After that he
kept me up there for weeks. It was only this morning that he
turned me loose, and when I came down here on my way out
of this country the things began to happen that you know about.
And that's the truth, so help me God!"

He paused. And there was a heavy silence over the listeners.
The vigor of his speech had won him some belief.

"Why he done it," said Jack, "why he didn't kill me to get
even for the killing of Charlie, I dunno. Maybe you folks can
figure it out, for a gent that has this scar on his forehead seems
to be worse'n a ghost to the rest of you."

A muttering assent reached his ears. Susan, who had been
kept away by the jostling circle of men now found a way to
break through and came up to him, snorting. Captain Carney
picked upon that incident.

"Look at that, boys," he said. "I guess a gent that has a hoss
trained like that ain't all snake. I say, we're going to listen to
some more that this gent has to say. You say you ain't Charlie
Sherry?"

"I'm not."

"What might your name be, then?"

"Jack Bristol."

"And where might you come from, Jack?"

"From down Arizona way."

"The hell you say! All that ways to up here?"

"That's the straight of it, Carney."

"How come you to make a trip as long as that? Just started
out to see a piece of the country?"

Jack paused to consider.

"Fact is," he admitted, at length, "that I got into a scrape down yonder. I had to get out and get out quick, and the best thing for me was to get as far away as I could. So I started north and never stopped until old Hank Sherry got his paws on me!"

"That sounds like queer talk to me," said Carney, "but it sounds like the sort of talk that a gent wouldn't make up in a minute. What d'ye say, boys? Ain't there a sound of truth in what he says?"

A dubious, but growing chorus of assent answered him. Then a big man appeared from the background and shouldered his way to the front.

"Boys," said the voice of Lee Jarvis, "you've been hearing a good deal of strange talk. If you'll let me ask this fellow a few questions, I'll guarantee that I'll show you his guilt. Will you let me ask them?"

CHAPTER X

"IT'S LEE Jarvis," said Captain Carney ingratiatingly. "I guess we can listen to Oliver Jarvis' son, boys? Step up and talk to him, Jarvis."

"Thank you, Captain," said the other, and came into the little circle which was now occupied by brown Susan, Jack, and the captain.

"In the first place," he began, "I don't mind telling you why I'm interested. This infernal blackguard rode up behind me, held me up, took my wallet, and then struck me in the face with his revolver and knocked me senseless. Then he went on and met Nell Carney and told her that he was a messenger from me."

"By God!" cried Jack, "that's the grandfather of all the lies that were ever told!"

"I've got proof to show you," said Lee Jarvis.

And he calmly lighted a match and held it cupped so that the light would fall upon his face. It showed to Jack the complete story of the work which he had done with his fists and he found that story to be far more extensive than he had imagined. The mouth of Jarvis was puffed and bloody. A purple bruise decorated his chin. There was a red gash under one eye and the other was nearly closed by a discolored swelling. Moreover, his face, his hair, and his clothes were covered with unbrushed dust.

A murmur ran through the crowd at the sight.

"Does it look as though one blow had done all that?" asked Jack of the crowd. "Tell them the truth, Jarvis—that we stood up and fought a square fight till you went down!"

"You lying rascal," said the bigger man, though he kept his voice admirably under control. "You know that I fell head foremost from my saddle and struck on rocks by the road! But we'll put that to one side. What was in his mind about Nell Carney, God alone knows. She's safe at home; how she got there we'll find out later on."

The quiet and assured manner in which Lee Jarvis uttered his misstatements staggered even Jack, and it was plain that they made a great impression upon the others.

"Now," went on Lee Jarvis, "we'll ask you a few simple questions. In the first place, what was the crime on account of which you were forced to run for your life from Arizona?"

"There's nothing I've done there which has anything to do with what I have done here."

"Answer me yes or no!" exclaimed Jarvis. "Did you or did you not kill a man in Arizona before you started north?"

The picture of Harry Ganton lying on the floor of his house flashed back upon the mind of Jack.

"I'll not answer that," he said.

"You're doing yourself a harm," said Captain Carney sternly. "If you could have actually established that you were in Arizona, of course it would have proved that you are not Charlie Sherry. You understand that?"

To be hanged for the murder of Sheriff Ganton, or to be lynched by a mob here—what difference was there between those fates? Jack shrugged his shoulders.

"Let's go back," said Lee Jarvis, "to the yarn which he has just told."

He planted himself squarely before Jack, his hand dropped upon his hips.

"When you saw the cross on the forehead of the old man," he asked, "of course you asked what it meant?"

"I did not," said Jack, "and I still don't know what it means."

"Shall I tell him, then?" said Lee Jarvis. "Shall I let him in on the secret?"

"Go ahead," said Carney.

"Well, Charlie Sherry," said Jarvis, "we understand that you know it well enough, but I'll tell it to you over again. It goes back to a time when your father was living in this valley and when you were a little shaver, you and your three brothers. Hank Sherry was always the black sheep of the community. The Sherry family, as a matter of fact, had always been the black sheep. They'd raised hell in one way or another for a couple of generations. If there was ever a theft, or a horse-stealing, or a murder in the community, it was always safe to hunt up the Sherrys, in the first place. Because the crime was, nearly always, traced back to one of them. Finally the crowning horror came. Fire broke out in the house of the minister one night. Everyone in the valley knew the minister. He'd put his shoulder under every man's troubles, at one time or another. He had slaved up and down the length of the valley for thirty years doing good. He'd married a girl in the valley; he'd raised a family of three children late in life.

"Fire, as I say, broke out in the minister's house. It began with the explosion of a revolver. When neighbors ran out into the street they found the minister shouting, "Stop thief," and pointing down the street and crying that Oscar Sherry had robbed his house. But the crowd could not chase your uncle. They had work closer at hand.

"In his flight, to distract the attention of the minister, the thief had thrown a burning lamp upon the floor of the house. The oil washed the fire across the floor. Instantly the lower part of the house was on fire.

"It was an old house. The fire spread wonderfully fast. When the minister turned to go back into his house, after he had chased the thief out, his way up the stairs was blocked with the flames. And his wife and three children were cut off from help above. I remember that night, and the crowd in the street, and the way the men fought the fire and tried to get through to the family."

A groan arose from the crowd. They pressed a little closer. There were older men in that assemblage who had actually fought the flames on that night.

"But they couldn't keep the fire down with their bucket lines," went on Lee Jarvis, "and finally one of the children began screaming upstairs and the minister couldn't stand it. He ran through the flames and got upstairs. And that was the last of him. A minute later the upper floor caved in. The walls of the house held in a furnace and the minister's family perished in it, five of them died there, Charlie Sherry!"

In the pause Jack heard the heavy breathing of the men who surrounded him.

"Afterward," went on Lee Jarvis, "they hunted down the Sherrys, as usual, and they found the plunder from the minister's house in the home of Oscar Sherry.

"That was enough. Oscar Sherry was lynched and hung to the highest tree in the village. He died cursing the rest of the world. And after his death the men of the valley decided that something had to be done to get rid of the curse of the Sherry family. And they decided to send them out of the valley, Hank Sherry and his four sons, and mark them all so that they could never come back without being known. It was a stern thing to do, but five deaths had just been laid to the door of the Sherry family, and there were other murders—a long list of 'em—stretching back over the years. So a band of masked men took your father and the four of you—think back to that night, Charlie!—and they branded a cross on the forehead of each of you and then sent you out of the valley with a warning that if any one of you ever came back again he'd be killed!

"And they did come back. Five years ago a horse thief was caught at Lower Falls. There was a cross branded on his forehead. On him were found the wallet and the watch of a man who had been murdered on the road three days before. The thief and murderer admitted that he was Mike Sherry, the oldest of your brothers.

"Six months later there was a highway robbery. The robber was run down by a posse. He killed Tom Evans before he was captured and when he was caught the posse found a cross on his forehead and he gave his name as Gus Sherry.

"The next was only ten months ago. Jud Sherry came down into the valley and tackled Hal Sewell. But Hal was lucky with his gun and dropped the murderer in his tracks.

"Last of all, here you come, Charlie—the smoothest liar of the lot. All of your brothers have shown the same poison in their blood. They've all been raised, like you, to hate the rest of the world. And we caught them all in murders, or on the edge of murders. And we finished every one of them just as we're going to finish you, Charlie Sherry! Boys, am I right?"

"Right!" they answered.

One voice opposed.

"Not right enough to suit me," said Captain Carney. "I've got to hear more than that. You've framed up an ugly story, Jarvis. But where's the facts?"

"Facts?" said Jarvis fiercely. "What he did to me is one fact. Not a doubt in the world that he thought I was dead and that he left me for that reason."

"Search him for the wallet," said the captain. "That will be proof enough."

Matches were lighted. Busy hands probed the pockets of Jack's coat, and "Here!" cried one. "Here it is!"

Before the amazed eyes of Jack was exposed a thin wallet which had been drawn from his pocket. The leather case was opened. A thin sheaf of bills was exposed.

"All twenties and bigger," said Captain Carney. "Not a bad haul for him, at that."

"Is that proof enough now?" asked Lee Jarvis.

"Hang him! Send him to hell and be done with him!" was

the loudly voiced consensus of opinion, but Captain Carney still held them back with the weight of his single opinion, as a strong and honest man can often do, even with thousands. All around Jack Bristol they swayed and stirred. But Carney was steady as a rock.

"Wait a minute," he commanded. "This shows that he robbed you. That's the sort of a thing that a Sherry might do. But it ain't proof that he is a Sherry."

"Captain," exclaimed Lee Jarvis, "you're arguing flatly on his side. I've proved the robbery. And now you see the scar. It's simply blind obstinacy to doubt any longer!"

He added, "I'll show you one thing more."

He lighted another match and held it so that the light gleamed in the eyes of Jack.

"Look at that scar. Does it seem like a new one? It's an old, white scar, Carney!"

"If that wound got good care, it might look like that inside of a few weeks. There's no proof in what you say now, Jarvis."

"No proof in any one thing I've said, but there's a lot of proof when the entire number are strung together. What speaks up for him?"

"Two things," said Carney. "The first is that he keeps silent. That's a good thing. No whining. No begging. No matter what else he may be, he's a man, Jarvis."

He waited a moment for that point to sink home.

"The second thing is: why did he ride home with Nell? I only had ten seconds to hear her yarn but from what she said I gathered that he talked like a decent fellow. How do you explain that, Jarvis?"

"Leave it to a vote of the crowd," suggested Jarvis.

The malignance of the man astonished Jack, though the explanation could be found in his desire to get rid of a man who had beaten and shamed him.

"I've got one thing to say," said Jack at length, before the roar of the crowd had begun calling for the end of him. "Take a guard and bring me up to face Hank Sherry. If he calls me his son, that'll settle it. Is that fair?"

"A fifteen mile ride through the hills to prove a thing we already know?" stormed Lee Jarvis. "Why should we do that?"

"Because there's a man's life balanced in this," answered Carney. "And that's the thing that we're going to do. I'll ride in the morning. Jarvis, I'll count on having you along. Pat, Steve, Joe, will you ride up with us?"

He carried them before him. The objections of Lee Jarvis were over-ruled. In five minutes the posse which was to ride in the morning was formed, and it was agreed who should guard the prisoner during that night.

CHAPTER XI

I N T H E   first cold gray of the morning they came to Jack
Bristol in the cellar room of the Carney house where he was
being guarded. A cup of black coffee and a piece of bread with
a couple of slices of bacon on top made the breakfast. And a
little later they started up the valley with brown Susan dancing
gaily on the way while her rider was held in the noose of a lariat
which was twisted around the horn of Carney's saddle.

Jack looked back at the house and he saw, in a window which
opened just above the roof of the veranda, the face of Nell
Carney watching him depart, with a strained expression of
loathing and terror. His hands were lashed together, but he
raised them both and lifted his sombrero to her. She disappeared
to the side at once and Jack, as he settled the hat back on his
head with a grim smile, saw Carney himself eyeing him with
a measure of grim interest, but not a word was spoken.

It was plain, however, that whatever Nell had told her father,
she had not completely prejudiced him against her escort of
the night before, for all during the ride Captain Carney rode
near the prisoner. It was at his suggestion that the rope was
removed from Jack and attached merely to the neck of Susan.
And above all, something in his manner was a steady assurance
to Jack that in a pinch there was one man in the posse who
would see that some measure of justice was meted out to the
captive.

As for the others in the group, riding before and behind Jack,

they maintained a resolute silence, so far as the man they
guarded was concerned. They avoided even looking at him, as
though they feared that if they met his glance they would have
to recognize him as a human being worthy of mercy, at least.
So grim was their mood that even when they spoke to one
another it was in lowered voices.

So they worked their way quickly out of the valley before
the morning fires began smoking in the chimneys they passed.
They were entering the hills before, looking back, Jack saw a
dozen ghostly and wavering fingers of smoke rising. The valley
was still half lost in dimness, but the crests above them were
already brightening with the sun. The sun itself came gleaming
over an eastern mountain as the posse rode into view of the
Sherry cabin.

They heard him before they saw him. An ax was swinging
lustily somewhere below them, where the roof of the cabin was
visible, and with every blow the thin and tempered steel rang
loudly. Captain Carney bent his head to one side and listened
with a critical air.

"That's a good ax man," he said. "He's sinking her up to the
wood every wallop, pretty near. That's old Hank Sherry himself,
I should say. He was always fast with an ax."

Jack Bristol, fresh from the land where wood is dug up rather
than chopped down, listened to the opinion with wonder. And
now they heard a crackling and rustling among the trees near
the cabin. Next, with a rush like a great wind, down rushed a
huge pine and fell crashing and splintered. The steep hills caught
up the echoes and sent them flying off into faint distances. Then
the riders came into view of the woodsman. It was Hank Sherry,
of course. He leaned upon his ax and, wiping the sweat from
his forehead, looked down upon the white stump, glistening
with the chisel strokes of the ax and bristling in the center with
a tuft of splintered wood.

But at sight of the approaching procession, he tossed the ax
far to one side and ran upon them with a cry of agony. He ran

straight to Jack, and though one or two of the riders laid hands upon guns, they offered no resistance. The odds were too safe upon their side.

"Charlie!" cried the old villain, taking hold of Jack's imprisoned hands. "Oh, God A'mighty, I knew it would come out like this! You shouldn't have gone down into the valley. I begged you and I prayed you not to go. I knew they'd get you. There's a curse on us down yonder. And now they've brought you up here to hang you before my eyes—"

He bowed his head into his hands and rested his forehead against the neck of Susan. And the bright-eyed mare turned and sniffed kindly at his shoulder.

As for Jack, he was utterly stunned. Only dimly his mind began to grope toward an understanding of the mountaineer, if indeed Hank Sherry had schemed so elaborately simply to have the slayer of his son hung by the citizens of the valley. And now Lee Jarvis, who had kept carefully in the background and offered not a single opinion during the journey, pressed forward. In the morning light all the bruises of the battle of the night before showed plainly. One eye was half shut and the other swollen, giving a strangely sleepy cast to his expression. That sleepiness was belied by the timbre of his voice. It was plain to Jack that shame and rage had worked together in Jarvis until he was in a murderous passion.

"With all due respect to you, Captain," he said to Carney, "I imagine that this proves what I've been arguing about. Yonder is a tree with a conveniently horizontal branch. We have half a dozen ropes with us. Why not finish the business at once? I suppose there is no more argument about whether or not he's the son of Hank Sherry?"

"Carney," said Jack, "so help me God, you're doing a murder if you let this go through. I'm not Charlie Sherry. He was a bigger man by two inches. I haven't had a chance to shave. This beard has grown out and made me look more like him. My hair and eyes are black like his. What this hound, Sherry, has been driving at, I don't know. But part of it seems to me that he wants to get me hung as his son!"

"Get him hung?" exclaimed Hank Sherry, stepping back and looking wildly around at the posse. "Gents, gimme a chance to buy him. No matter what he's stolen, I'll try to pay for it. Or if he's hurt somebody, then take me instead of him. Gents, he's all that's left to me! You've taken the other three. You've killed 'em one by one. I don't say it wasn't justice. I don't accuse none of you. I don't say it was done without no court approving of what you done to 'em. But I say, for God's sake, friends, let me have this last one! Carney, you've got a daughter!"

"Stop this damned noise," said Carney loudly. "Jarvis, you're right. Something has been holding me back. I don't know what. There is a queer, straight look about the eyes of this fellow that's not at all like the look of the other Sherrys. But of course it has been proved six times over. This is Charlie Sherry. And he hangs for it. Steve, throw your rope over that branch, will you? We'll get the dirty business ended."

Steve, a leather-skinned and much wrinkled cowpuncher of middle-age, looked down upon his rope as though he pitied it the horrible duty which it was to perform. Then, with the utmost dexterity he shot the noosed end over the designated branch. Jack Bristol followed that movement with dull eyes. His mind refused to understand. He found himself noting more than the dangling rope, the singing of a bird in the higher branches, and the fragrance of the pines, and the brightness of the sun as it fell, brilliant but without warmth, into the glade. Even the bustle of the cowpunchers closing in upon him conveyed no meaning to him. But here Hank Sherry pressed in before him, facing Captain Carney. And as he came in, Jack felt a slight tug at the rope which bound his hands together. He looked down in time to see the quick glint of a knife disappearing with open blade into the deep hip pocket of Hank's trousers. A deft backhand stroke had severed the rope in one place. It only remained for Jack to loosen and shake off the rest of the rope and he would be free. But in order to escape he would have to gain the back of Susan, it seemed, and since he had been dismounted only the moment before at the command of Carney, while Steve was throwing the rope over the branch, the difficulty was almost insuperable. But the parting of the rope had roused an instant hope in him. A slight turning of his wrists caused the entire length of the rope to loosen. At any instant he could shake it off. But in the meantime he flashed a glance over the others.

No hand was near a weapon. They were rather intent upon the length of swinging rope and upon the plea of Hank Sherry. For the strange old man had thrown himself upon his knees beside Carney's horse, and reaching up both of his grimy hands, he was shrieking forth an appeal that they spare "Charlie, my boy, the last that's left to me—"

Here a hand fell rudely upon the shoulder of Jack, and he looked up into the face of Lee Jarvis.

"Over under the tree," said Jarvis, fairly trembling with fierce satisfaction. "That's your place. That fool's howling won't save you!"

He thrust Jack forward and the latter went without resistance and took his place where the noose of the rope touched against his cheek. Around him stood the horses of the posse in loose circle. And beyond the horses, behind the big tree from which the rope hung, the mountainside rose at a sheer angle covered with a dense second growth. In the meantime, the voice of Hank Sherry had risen still louder.

"Say, Joe," protested Carney, "will you give me a hand to take the poor old devil away to his house and lock him up until this is over?"

Joe started his horse obediently forward. It passed between Jack and Carney, and at that instant Jack shook the rope from his wrist and sprang away for safety. There was no safe interval between the horses immediately in front of him. Instead of attempting to slide through, he dived under Steve's horse, which stood with its side presented. And while the latter whipped out his revolver with a startled yell, Jack rolled to his feet on the very edge of the dense forest of second-growth trees.

Half a dozen guns exploded almost at the same instant behind him, but there was only a pin prick at his left shoulder and the next moment he had leaped behind the screen of leaves. Once there he ducked down and ran as close to the earth as possible, not up the steep hillside, but cutting across close to the edge of the clearing. And that maneuver saved his life for the moment, at least. Carney and Steve had sent their horses crashing up the mountainside through the saplings and, with the aid of the others, searched the ground before them with a steady fusillade of revolver bullets. A headlong flight would have ended, for Jack, in ten seconds. But running to the side the noise of his feet on crackling twigs fully covered by the shouting of the posse, the roar of guns, the snorting of horses, he skirted the clearing and came, in this fashion, to a point a hundred yards away.

There he looked out and saw Lee Jarvis gathering the reins of brown Susan. At least the big man knew a fine horse and had picked for himself the cream of the spoils of war. The sharp whistle of Jack brought Susan forward with a bound. The reins whipped out of the hands of Jarvis and tugged him forward. His toe struck a root and he toppled on his face while Susan came flying. She slackened her pace, but did not stop for Jack. There was no need. He sprang for the saddle, clung with foot and hand like a cat, and with a hail of lead whistling about him, gained the back of the mare and twisted into temporary safety among the trees at the same instant.

He looked back, as he flicked out of sight. The riders were storming across the clearing at full speed. Had they shot from a stand they must have riddled him with bullets. But they were following the lead of the old instinct which bids a man charge home and get to close quarters.

But they never sighted him in pistol shot again. Riding flattened to the back of Susan, letting her weave among the trees at her own will, Jack drew swiftly away until they came into an open natural lane among the trees, and down this the mare fled with arrowy swiftness. Once again, topping a bare shoulder of a mountain, Jack looked back and saw the others flogging their mounts ahead. But the random volley which they raised fell short and Jack turned in the saddle and waved a mocking farewell as he dipped out of sight again.

CHAPTER XII

HE DID not drive straight away from those unlucky
mountains. No. Culver Valley and the worthy inhabitants
thereof had by no means heard the last of Jack Bristol. He
allowed Susan to travel on for less than an hour. Then he turned
her to one side over a stretch of rock where she could not be
trailed with any ease or speed, unbridled her on a grassy mead-
owland, and let her graze till noon without sighting any of the
pursuers. Doubtless that first taste of the mare's running powers
had convinced hard-headed Carney and the rest that a pursuit
straight across the mountains would be worse than useless, so
they had winded.

And when the sun hung high at noon, Jack bridled the mare
again and turned straight back on the trail from which he had
come. He wanted first to corner Sherry and learn from that
mysterious-minded fellow exactly what had been going on in
his brain. And after that there were certain duties which he
wished to perform in Culver Valley. For they had made him
taste all the agony of death; and against that heavy account he
wished to pile up a balance.

He used little care during his approach to the Sherry house.
He was reasonably sure that the disappointed posse would not
wait patiently in the clearing. They would not dream that he
dared return so soon. And they would go back to the valley to
spread their unhappy tidings and warn the inhabitants along
the Culver River to beware of the vengeance which was im-

pending. It would be strange indeed if armed parties did not ride up and down the valley roads that night!

So he came back to the edge of the clearing and looked out from a gap in the trees. There was no sign of hostile life. Only a column of smoke rose lazily from the chimney. It was all so peaceful, with the noonday sun pressing hot upon the clearing, that it seemed impossible he had been a few seconds from death there that morning.

He cantered Susan boldly to the door of the cabin and dismounted. There stood Hank Sherry at the stove, a sack tied around his hips by way of an apron, frying meat, the fragrance of which rolled heavily to the nostrils of hungry Jack Bristol. The big mountaineer turned slowly, juggling a fork idly in his hand after the fashion of a cook. He nodded to Jack without the slightest sign of surprise.

"Sit down," he said. "Chuck is about ready."

He pointed, and Jack saw that the table was equipped for two! He shied his sombrero across the room.

"Sherry," he said, "I ought to salt you away with lead. But by God, I ain't got the heart to pull a gun on you! I ought to cut that lying tongue of yours out of your head and nail it in the sun to dry. But the lies that tongue told this morning helped give me a chance to break away. There's only one bargain I'm going to strike with you: Tell me what hellishness was in your mind at the start of all this. Will you do that?"

"And if I don't?" said the mountaineer, scowling terribly upon him.

"If you don't," said Jack calmly. "I'll stake you out on that clearing with your face turned up to the sun."

The other shrunk back.

"I'm an old man," he said. "I'm a pretty old man, Jack. Would you treat me like that?"

"Has an old wolf got any call over a young wolf?" said Jack.

He was astonished to see the other nod and actually smile,

as though he were pleased by the ultimatum which Jack had delivered.

"Sit down and eat," he said mildly.

"Have I been asking you a question?" said Jack. "Or maybe was it a chickadee singing on a stick?"

The mountaineer laughed uproariously.

"Son," he said, "you sure have a way with you. Well, I'll tell you everything you want to know. But sit down and eat first."

"Why?" said Jack. "I'll hear you talk before I eat."

"You won't," said the other with an equal firmness. "Because what I've got to say will be bad enough to hear on a full stomach, but it'd sure get me a filling of lead if I talked to you hungry. Keep a bear's belly full and the bear ain't going to bother you none. I've handled game before, son!"

It was impossible, for some reason, to stand up before the assurance of the trapper. He stood with his hands resting on his hips, squinting out at Jack through his red-shaded eyes with an expression of exhaustless evil will.

So Jack Bristol sat down and took his place in friendly fashion opposite Sherry, his fascinated eyes never leaving the white cross in the forehead of the mountaineer, never ceasing to remember that the same brand was in his own flesh. And even against his will and against his conscious mind, it constituted a strong bond between them.

Not that he for an instant relaxed his guard. No, every instant he was sternly on watch for some trickery on the part of the older man. He sat in such a position that he could keep his eye upon the door. At any moment some unknown ally of Hank Sherry, he felt, might break in upon him. And yet, under the attitude of Sherry it was not violent hatred which he sensed. It was, rather, a profound determination to show a better side to him. The friendliness of the mountaineer surrounded him.

"Sherry," said Jack suddenly, "what do you expect me to do?"

"I got no expectations," answered Hank calmly.

"What d'you mean by that?"

"I mean, I don't know which way you're going to jump. You may go at my throat, or agin you may sit there real sensible and eat what I'm cooking for you. I dunno which you'll do."

In spite of himself, Jack felt a smile beginning somewhere in him. Only in waves, now and again, he recalled the old hatred of his former jailer. But the manner of Sherry seemed to banish all that had happened into the unimportant past. Again he told himself that he could not harm a man so much older than he; and also, he assured himself that to take revenge upon Hank Sherry now would be like taking revenge upon a wild beast for acting as nature teaches it to act. Opposed to this was a faint, but growing suspicion that Sherry was less beast and more man than he had suspected all the time he had been there.

"Hank," he said at last, "tell me what's been in your head and what you got planned for me now."

The mountaineer shrugged his shoulders.

"What I got planned for you?" he queried.

"You knew what would happen to me when I left. What is your plan?"

"If I was to tell you the whole of it," said Hank Sherry, "it would be a lot better if I could show you what I was talking about. Suppose we climb up yonder and get a peek at the whole of Culver Valley?"

Jack Bristol nodded and followed up the mountainside. He was more and more profoundly amazed by the manner in which Sherry dominated him. He had every reason to wish to destroy the mountaineer. He had been tortured and branded and his very identity changed by this strange and terrible old man, but behold! he had just risen from the same table with Hank Sherry and now walked up the mountainside meekly submissive to the will of his leader.

While he turned these thoughts in his head, they struggled up the mountainside until they reached the crest. The climb had been as steep as a ladder, and they had risen to the bald summit above timberline. Unobstructed by trees, the vision swept clear before them over a host of lower peaks.

"And yonder," said Hank Sherry, pointing, "is Culver Valley!"

It was spread out neatly before them. The distance compacted it like a map so that the eye caught every feature at a single glance, and the marvelous clearness of the mountain air kept every detail clear. Culver Valley was funnel-shaped, running out from between loftier mountains near at hand and extending toward lower and lower hills as it grew wider until its mouth was lost in the horizon mist far away. And in the center they saw the bright streak of the Culver River twisting out toward the plains beyond.

"There it is," said Hank Sherry, "there she lies—old Culver Valley!"

Jack, looking at his guide in surprise at the emotion in his voice, saw Hank Sherry raise his hand and pass it slowly across his forehead, as though to shield his eyes from what they saw, or to erase some torturing memory from his mind.

"It's the first time in all these years," said Hank. "It's the first time that I've ever looked at Culver Valley. But there ain't been a day that I ain't thought about it. I've stayed down yonder in that cabin and told myself that I'd forget all about everything I'd lost. But it's a pile harder to do things than it is to say 'em. Every time I've looked up here at the top of this mountain, I knew damn well what the mountain was seeing, and it was like a mirror to me. I looked to the mountain and the mountain showed me clear as glass all that I'd lost, all that they'd robbed me of. And it ain't changed. It's just exactly the way that I expected it to be. There's Bleak Mountain standing north—my God, I've seen Bleak Mountain on better days than this! I've seen him wrapped up in rain-fog on the day that my first boy was born. I've seen every tree on his sides on the clear morning that I was married. Yes, sir, there's old Bleak Mountain! Lord God, son, it's a queer thing how we're all tied up with the things that we've seen. I've looked at Bleak Mountain so often that it seems to me that Bleak Mountain must have eyes to look back at me. I've been happy and blue so many times, when I rode under the shadow of Bleak Mountain that damned if I ain't got to feel that the mountain was happy and blue just the same as me!"

He paused and shook his head, while Jack Bristol looked upon him with a deeper amazement than ever. A peculiar gentleness had come over the voice and the eye of the veteran in this moment. He lost in grimness; he gained in kindly dignity.

"Damn their rotten souls," snarled Hank Sherry. "I'll see 'em all in hell one of these days if only I could help to put 'em there!"

The kindliness was gone; in a flash there was nothing but black malice in all his nature. But he added after an instant, "And there Culver Mountains running south, and there's the old Culver River in the middle. Why, son, it brings me jump into the middle of the days when I was a youngster, younger'n you, spry as a linnet, full of hell-fire and happiness!"

He stretched out his long, heavy arms and then let them fall to his sides.

"That's finished," he said. "Well," he added, turning to Jack with another alteration of expression, "I ain't brought you up here to talk about scenery. I come up here to talk to you about the kind of folks that live down yonder in that valley!" He paused.

"Might it be," he said as he began to speak again, "that when you were down yonder they told you something about me and my boys and how we come to be marked?"

"I heard that all from Lee Jarvis," said Jack.

"Jarvis, and it was his father that done the suggesting! It was his father that led the way and the rest of 'em followed. Well, I know that they told you—about the burning of the minister's house, and how they found out that my brother, Oscar, was the thief, and how they decided to mark the Sherrys and get rid of 'em, and how many years they'd stood for what the Sherrys had done in Culver Valley. They told you all of that?"

"They did," admitted Jack, and he looked curiously at the big man, wondering what counter claim he could put up to justify his blood.

"When I begun to grow up," said Hank Sherry, "it wasn't hard for me to tell that other folks wasn't particular fond of me. If it happened that there was any whispering or noise-making or foolishness in school, the teacher didn't hesitate more'n a minute. She come straight down to my seat and yanked me up and licked me for what I'd never done. Same way through all the rest of the town. If anything went wrong they come looking for me or for brother Oscar.

"Well, son, you can't keep tar around all the time without getting dirty now and then. When I begun to get a little bit older and big enough to think for myself, I says, "As long as they think I'm bad, why not be bad? As long as they figure me to be a sneak and a thief and no good, why not get the fun of doing the things that they think I'm doing?"

He paused again and walked a pace up and down the brow of the mountain, and still Jack stared at him with an immense curiosity. It seemed perfectly incredible that any moral considerations had ever influenced the brain beneath that slant and brutal forehead.

"Well," went on the mountaineer, "I begun to do what they expected of me. My brother, Oscar, had started long before, and he showed me the way. For a couple of years I raised hell in one way or another pretty steady, but then I got a shock. I met up with a girl that had come new to the town with a pair of big, black eyes and a smile that stopped you up like a jerk on a Spanish bit and a laugh that kept echoing inside of you. Ever meet up with a girl like that?"

"Yes," said Jack Bristol, and the picture of Nell Carney rose in his mind and took the place of the portrait which Sherry had drawn.

"I met that girl," went on Sherry, "and she knocked me loose from my old way of living. I didn't see nothing but her. She filled up the whole sky for me. I went to sleep thinking about her. I woke up dreaming about her. And I went hunting her, you might say. Well, she was new to the town, she hadn't hardly had a chance to learn the truth about me, and because she seen so much of me to begin with, she got to sort of liking me. Then along comes young Jarvis, that's the father of the Lee Jarvis that you know. He was the richest man in Culver Valley. And when he seen my girl he sure lost his head. Because all the Jarvis men go wild when they see a pretty face. And the first thing that skunk done was to go sneaking to her and tell her all about what the Sherry family stood for in Culver Valley!"

He ground his teeth as he remembered.

"It made her sick to listen to him, but the first thing she done after hearing was to come straight to me and tell me everything. And out of her telling me what she'd heard, and out of me admitting part of it and what not, the short of it was that we got married the same day, me because I loved the ground she walked on, and her because she thought she could save me from being what all my family had been before me.

"And she did save me, partner. We had four sons. I kept her comfortable and happy. I built a house; I got it fixed up; when I hired out to work I done more'n any two men. And when she died, I just kept right on because every one of them four boys had something of her in 'em. One had her happy way of talking and laughing all together, and another of 'em had the ways of her head and hand, and Charlie had her eyes. He had her eyes exactly!"

Here he paused again and once more made a turn up and down on the brow of the mountain, while Jack Bristol pitied him with all his heart.

"The boys growed up," said Hank Sherry, "and they got what I'd got before them. They got what everybody by the name of Sherry is always sure to get in Culver Valley. They was suspected when they did nothing. They couldn't go out and play in the street without having grown folks come out and keep an eye on 'em. And when the boys got a bit old it riled 'em bad to see the way they got treated. But I kept a stiff rein on 'em. I kept 'em straight, d'ye see? I worked like hell myself; I kept 'em working, too. They learned their lessons in school; they done their work; they didn't bother other folks. But still, in spite of that, nobody trusted 'em. Because there was the long years the Sherrys had always been bad, and there was my brother Oscar right then spending most of his time in jail.

"Then along come the time when the minister's house was burned. God knows I didn't have no hand in the burning of that house. That minister sure had the mercy of God in him. He was one man in town that believed in me. He was the one man in the whole of Culver Valley that would come and sit down with me and wish me luck! When I heard the fire alarm, I went and I worked with the first of 'em. It was me that stood first in the bucket line until the heat of the fire peels the skin off of my face. And then when I went off, near fainting, I was so plumb done up, the roof crashed in and I heard 'em say that the whole family was wiped out.

"It was as though one of my own boys had been killed in that fire. I went home all sick inside. And then they come and got us out of bed, all of us, and me with the bandages still on my face where the fire had burned me. They got us out and they told us they'd hanged Oscar for the minister's death. And then they lined up the boys and heated a poker red-hot, white-hot—"

He stopped again and tore his shirt open at the throat. Jack himself felt as though he were half stifled.

"They took my biggest son first. They held him down. And while he screamed they sent the iron smoking on his forehead. And it was Jarvis who held the poker. Oh, God, am I ever going to forget that?"

He cast up his great arms as though with a blasphemous defiance against the heavens.

"Then they heated the poker again and they got the other three boys, one after another. Last of all they come to Charlie.

He was only a little shaver then. I got down on my knees to them and begged, but Jarvis damned me and branded little Charlie with the rest. And then they come to me. But I didn't feel the iron. There was too much pain on the inside of me to feel a thing like that. I saw the smoke of my own flesh roll in front of my eyes. That was about all. And then I looked at my boys and I knew that their lives were ruined."

His voice changed.

"I still had a hope. I thought that I could make my boys grow up honest and straight. What was a mark in the skin, after all? Nothing terrible bad. Nothing that couldn't be lived down, I hoped. So I took them up here in the mountains and we built a house and lived by ourselves and trapped and hunted and got along pretty fine.

"And then one day a hunting party come up from the Culver Valley. And they come upon one of my boys in the hills. There was a pretty girl riding out ahead. When she seen the mark on his forehead she lets out a scream, and the rest of 'em come galloping up. They seen the mark on his forehead, too. They didn't ask no questions. They took it for granted that he'd tried to harm her, and they tied him to a tree and quirted him till the blood run down his back.

"He came back home. That night my two oldest boys sat down with him and they swore that they'd be even with the rest of the world for what had been done to 'em. I begged 'em not to try to fight odds of a million to one, but they went ahead, anyway. And one by one I lost 'em. Only Charlie remained. He was the best of the lot, and I thought that he'd get to be a fine man. And then you come, and he sees that mare and wants her more'n anything else on earth. And the end of it was that he starts in to finish you. Mind you, it wasn't that he was bad by nature. But every time he seen himself in the mirror he said to himself that he was damned, anyway, no matter what he done! He couldn't come to no good end. And so, when he sees your hoss, he says to himself, "Why not?" So he went in, and you know the end of Charlie.

"Not that I blamed you, but I said to myself, "If they put a mark on me and my boys, and a curse on us along with the mark, why can't I pass the curse along to one of them and see what happens?" And that's why I done what I done. It was a terrible bad thing to do, son. I ain't denying that. But I seen for myself that you were a tiger at fighting, and the thought of turning a tiger loose in Culver Valley sure warmed the inwards of me. So I put the mark on you—and there's the end of the story."

He extended his right arm.

"Look down there. That's why I brought you up here. When Culver come here there was a Sherry with him. They split this valley in two and each took half. Along come the Jarvis folks. They cheated Culver out of his share. And now they've drove me out, and I'm the last Sherry!"

CHAPTER XIII

IT WAS a singular story, Jack decided, because it left all of the truly important things unsaid. It gave all of the causes and hinted only in a general way at the effect. It was said that he hoped to loose upon peaceful Culver Valley a tiger in the person of Jack Bristol. To that end he had stamped Jack with the indelible identity of a Sherry. But how could he be sure that Jack would accept the rôle which was prepared for him? Of that there was no doubt, because no matter where he went, he would be followed, sooner or later, by the news that he was a Sherry. And then he must return, if he cared at all for human sympathy, human converse, to the one soul in all the world who understood that he was free from blame.

But though the mountaineer left these things unsaid, they were patent and clear to Jack. Suddenly he put the question bluntly to his companion.

"But suppose, Sherry," he said, "that I light out on Susan and strike out a straight line until I get a thousand miles from here? Where does your plan go then?"

The other merely smiled and shook his head. As usual, he failed to look into the face of Jack, but stared into the vague distance while he answered.

"Suppose a wolf," said Hank Sherry, "never got hungry. Then it never would kill calves and colts, eh?"

"I don't foller you," said Jack.

"Well, they've rounded you up, ain't they?" said the mountaineer. "They've had a rope around your neck, so to speak, ain't they? They've showed you what the Culver Vigilantes are, ain't they? Ain't they talked to you about the Culver Vigilantes that never yet failed to get a gent that they started after? And after they've pretty nigh hanged you, d'you mean to say that you could go away without getting back at 'em?"

"And suppose that I do?" said Jack. "Lee Jarvis, I sure owe a grudge to. But after I get even with him, what's to keep me from leaving the valley and going on my way?"

"Why," said the other, "after you've started the game, maybe you'll find that it's too much fun to quit playing! But here's a chance for you to write all the lay of the land down in your head. If you was to go down into that valley, son, you'd have it alive and buzzing like a nest full of bees in a minute or two, son! They've got their telephones strung out everywhere. They shoot out of their alarms in a flock and they've got their damned vigilantes always ready to jump onto fast hosses with their guns and start out on a man hunt. They got a boast in Culver Valley that they don't need no sheriff. They take care of their own affairs"—his voice broke to a half-snarl, half-groan—"like they took care of me and my boys! So if you got a mind to take a crack at 'em, write all the roads and all the lay of the land in your brain, Jack."

There was no need to give that advice. Jack Bristol had already memorized every detail which could be seen in such a general survey. He was still continuing that mental survey as he returned down the hill with Hank Sherry. It was true. As Sherry had said, the temptation would be great. And the more he heard of the difficulty of the work, the more determined he was that Culver Valley had not yet heard the last of him. To be found in it again, of course, would mean instant death at the hands of whoever discovered him. To take that chance by entering the valley meant that he might have to shoot to kill in his own defense. But in spite of all dangers there was still a luring bait in the trap. Somewhere yonder in the valley was—yes, he had been able to pick out the very site of the Carney house—was

Nell, filled with horror to this moment by the thought that she had ridden alone through the night at the side of a Sherry.

All that remained of that afternoon Jack spent in grooming brown Susan and oiling a brace of revolvers and a rifle to be carried in a long holster under his knees when he rode. Hank Sherry paid not the slightest attention to him, but devoted himself to a continuation of his morning's labor of wood-chopping. His ax rang merrily and steadily until late afternoon with the sun just dropped behind the western mountains, and then it was that Jack Bristol set forth on his raid.

H E H A D only a vague purpose. On the one hand he must see Nell Carney and strive to convince her, before he left, that there was no stain in his blood. Then, having said farewell to her forever, he must find out Lee Jarvis, whose cruel cunning had brought him to the verge of death, find some means of striking at him a blow the rich man's son would never forget, and then ride on out of Culver Valley forever. As for the expectation of Hank Sherry that he could never disentangle himself from the pursuit of the Culver Vigilantes, he shrugged his shoulders at that evil prophecy.

Only in one respect had the mountaineer been right, and that was when he called the whole affair a game. A game it was, a truly wonderful game of chance. No game of cards was ever half so enthralling. For the stakes at cards could never run as high as life and death. He had played many a time for all his worldly possessions, but all of those former games were dull and stupid compared with this.

And as he went down the mountain pass into the upper levels of the Culver Valley, with the Culver River streaked down the center in a current of tarnished silver under the moon, a new happiness filled him. For there is no joy so keen as the joy of the fighter before he goes into battle. The ragged twinkling of lights in the lands below told him of so many homes, and in every home armed men ready to combat him. For he was the universal enemy. Yes, by the very fact that all hands were raised against him there was a suggestion that he possessed strength enough to combat them all.

Now brown Susan dropped into the smoother roads of the lowlands and the joyous rhythm of her gallop carried Jack on while the mountains rolled back farther and farther on either side; Bleak Mountain to the north and Culver Mountain on the south, rolling lines of summits dimly visible in the moonlight.

Hoofbeats drummed before him. Bobbing silhouettes of horsemen flocked on the road before him. But Jack Bristol kept straight on, sitting at an alert balance in the saddle, ready to flee, ready to fight. But by moonlight, who could recognize him?

The riders swept closer, dissolving from shadows into the distinct outlines of cowpunchers, with wide brims curling in the wind of their galloping, shouting to one another as they tore down the road. They had come in from some ranch among the hills.

They were starting for a "time." And speed was the best part of it all. They went by Jack with a chorus of whoops, and he answered them with shouts full as cheery. What would go through their brains if someone should tell them that they had just whipped past "Charlie Sherry?"

That thought set Jack laughing to himself as he went on. He overtook a buckboard with a pair of down-headed horses jogging slowly out the road. The driver called to him. He called joyously back to the driver. After all, these were not a peculiarly evil people. They simply saw in him a Sherry, and in the Sherrys they saw a clan who had brought destruction and terror to the Culver Valley. If he were among them, he would have shared all of their prejudices. That he knew.

And the result was that half of the venom was taken from his thoughts before he turned to the side and came down the lane which led to the house of Captain Carney. If he could only ride into town, give himself up, and demand that they send to the south for means of establishing his identity; if he could only do that, how pleasant it would then be, with scarred or unscarred forehead, to settle down and live the rest of his days in beautiful Culver Valley? But if they sent to the south they would establish his identity, so he thought, as the slayer of Sheriff Harry Ganton. Therefore there was nothing to do but see the girl for the last time, and then flee. Somewhere farther to the north there might be safety for him; somewhere far in the north and east in a cold country. A shiver went through him at the thought.

He found that the Carney house was lighted only in a front room and that not brilliantly. Telephone lines had been established in Culver Valley but there was not enough power to wire the houses with electricity. Therefore the windows were soft with yellow lamplight. He left Susan in the center of a small group of trees near the house and slipped up to observe what went on within that lighted room.

What he found was Nell Carney talking seriously with no less a personage than big Lee Jarvis.

CHAPTER XIV

I T WA S easy to see them and to hear. The shades were undrawn. He had only to ensconce himself at the side of the window opening upon the veranda in front of the house in order to both hear and see all that went on. And he eavesdropped shamelessly. Cruelty and bad luck had given him terrible handicaps in the matter of this girl. He felt that he could justifiably adopt somewhat shady methods in return.

"—and of course everything came out," Jarvis was saying. "The governor heard from a dozen sources about what had happened to me in my adventure with the Sherry blackguard. I waited in fear and trembling, Nell, upon my word! I thought that the old boy would descend upon me with lightning and thunder; because he was sure to guess that I was out to see you that night."

He laughed at the thoughts of his own fears. But while his head was raised, Jack noted that a faint sneer shadowed the lips of the girl for an instant and then disappeared. But still it seemed to Jack that she continued to observe her companion with a hawk-like fixity.

"You can imagine how I felt," ran on Jarvis, "when the old boy came in to see me and blurted out at once that he'd changed his mind. Anything I wanted as badly as I apparently wanted you, he thought would be all right. And marry you I should! And so, Nell, in five minutes everything was arranged! Can you believe it? Just when I thought that disaster had come along, the skies cleared and the sun shone on me; and next week, my dear, we'll be married, eh?"

He sprang from his chair as he spoke and went to her. Jack Bristol looked down in sudden agony.

"Good gad, Nell!" he heard Lee Jarvis exclaim, and looking up again, he saw that she had not stirred from her chair. But one partially lifted hand had stopped Jarvis in mid-stride.

"What's up?" gasped the big man. "You look cold as ice, Nell, confound me if you don't!"

"I'm sorry," said the girl. "I don't intend that. Only—"

"Well?"

"I don't know what it was," said the girl. "But when you came toward me like that I felt almost as if someone were watching us!"

She smiled faintly. Lee Jarvis, with an exclamation of annoyance, stepped closer to her. And looking up to him, she shrank back in what was almost absolute fear.

"Nell, what in the world has come over you? You look at me as though I were a stranger! You've acted like this ever since last night! Is it something I've done? Have I offended you? Don't be so infernally secretive. Try as I may, I never feel that I know more than the outer rim of your real nature!"

"I'm sorry," answered the girl, her voice falling to such a pitch that Jack could barely make out what she said. "I'm very sorry! But when you came toward me like that—well, Lee, I simply couldn't have endured it if you had taken me in your arms!"

He bit his lip.

"I know you've never liked that sort of thing," he said. "But good heavens, Nell, do you expect me to be a sort of old woman's companion and sit about and talk books, and what not?"

"I suppose that would be ridiculous, of course," said the girl with acid sarcasm that made Jarvis crimson. But she added at once in a kindlier tone, "Lee, we've always been more or less chums until your father sent you away to school. I missed you terribly when you were away. When you came back we were both so glad to see one another that don't you think we may have thought it was love, and after all there was not a bit of true love in our affection?"

His face was spotted with gray and purple, so sudden was the shock to him. One eye was now covered with a black patch. The other was discolored and squinting. For the instant his expression was one of devilish malevolence.

Then he turned on his heel and walked up and down the room for a turn or two without saying a word. And Jack could see that pride was battling in him and bidding him make no concession to her coldness. But his courage was not equal to his pride. He crumbled suddenly, and turning toward her cast out his hands.

"Good God, Nell, are you going to break things up?"

The girl rose in turn, and quickly, as though she had not realized until he spoke how very serious her last suggestion had been.

"I don't know what I've been saying, Lee," she said. "I—I haven't meant to hurt you—but—I—oh, of course I don't mean to break off anything unless you wish. I've given you my word, Lee, and my word is sacred. You surely know that!"

Lee Jarvis struggled with words that would not come, words which, Jack Bristol knew, should have assured her that he would never dream of holding her to her promise against her will. Then, on the gravel of the roadbed, there was a scattering of gravel and a horseman drew rein. Jack pressed closer to the side of the house, trusting to the shadow to conceal him. The stranger dismounted and came up to the front door.

"It's father," said Lee Jarvis with an air of immense relief. He lowered his voice and said something which Jack could not hear. Then he opened the door and a man as tall as young Jarvis and of the same cast of countenance entered. It was the same face, but grown older. The square outline was more pronounced. The jaw more square, and at its base little ridges of muscle leaped out when he set his teeth. The cheek-bones were high and made prominent by a spot of color upon them. The eyes were deep-set and extremely steady in their gaze. The whole frame of the man was big, well-filled, athletic. He bore his later middle-age resolutely and lightly. One would expect him to ride or walk as far as any agile youth. An indomitable will was stamped upon him. His step, his incisive manner of speech, his gestures, his reserve, were all typical of one sort of very strong man. Withal, he was a handsome man.

He stepped into the room, smiling and nodding to the girl. He shook hands with her and kept her hand in his for an instant. It seemed to Jack that he was examining her as something which was about to pass into the possession of his family. Perhaps the girl felt the same thing and it was this which made her flush.

"And everything is settled and a date arranged?" he suggested.

Young Jarvis stared at his fiancée in a very horror of alarm, but she answered his father with a smile of perfect assurance, "Next month is my lucky month, you see, and so we've decided to put it off at least as long as that."

"Very good," said the father, but there was a shadow on his face as he spoke. "I am not one who favors sudden action at any time other than a crisis. I'm about to go back to town just now because we have just passed through a trifling crisis!"

They murmured polite questions.

"Yes," said the elder Jarvis, his eyes sparkling, "someone let it out that there is a heavy deposit in cash in the Dexter Bank. And this evening there was an attempt to blow the door of the safe—"

A chorus of exclamations stopped him.

"I was walking down the street after dark," said the rich man of the Culver Valley, "and I caught a glint of light in the bank. It seemed odd to me. So I slipped across the street, opened the door with a pass key, and, to make a long story short, I bagged my man in the middle of his work, with his "soup", and "soap" laid out and only a few minutes' work left to him. It—"

"You fought him?" asked the son.

"It was a short fight. I knocked the rascal senseless and then tied his hands. When I got him out to a good light I recognized him as young Frank Stroud; from beggar to robber seems to be only a step!"

"Young Frank Stroud!" echoed the girl. "Poor fellow!"

The elder man turned sharply upon her.

"I presume that you have in mind," he said, "the story that I ground Frank's father between an upper and nether millstone and ground the life out of him, in the end. Is that's what's in your head, my dear? Let me tell you the truth. I found Frank Stroud senior a rich, but very foolish man. His business methods were slipshod. I often warned him against them, but he saw fit to go on his way disregarding my warnings. And the result was that when the crash came and I was in a position to clean him out, I did exactly that! I made him an example which will teach young men starting in business not to disregard advice!"

He stamped lightly as he spoke and set his teeth at the end of his speech so that hollows formed in his cheeks and a little wedge of muscle stood out at the base of his jaw.

"That's the story of Frank Stroud in brief. And now his son proves what the family is made of. The young wretch has turned into a professional safe-cracker. Well, he is lodged in the very front of the jail, now, and he can look through the bars at the bank which he tried to rob. The young fool begged like a dog to be let off. I laughed at him!"

And he laughed heartily, while Jack Bristol saw a flash of horror spread across the girl's face.

"But will you ride back with me?" suggested the father to the son. "I'll give you a look at young Stroud."

"I'd like that," grinned Lee Jarvis.

He turned away, in his excitement almost forgetful of Nell. She came to the door and watched them hurry out to their horses, and then the gravel was scattered in a flurry of hoofs as the two rushed away on the road for the town of Dexter and wretched Frank Stroud.

That noise of hoofs died out in the distance, was heard again as the face of a hill caught the passing sound and flung it back, and then the blessing of silence spread once more over the Culver Valley, a silence so complete that when the girl sighed as she stood at the door, it seemed to Jack that the sound was at his very ear.

CHAPTER XV

"YES," SAID Jack aloud, "I'd call it hard talk."

She gasped. The air swished around the door as she jerked it close. But it did not slam. Instead, she checked it and opened it again.

"Who is there?" she asked in a voice husky with fear.

"Somebody," said Jack, "who's on the outside of the house, and you're on the inside with fighting men ready to come on the jump the minute you call for 'em. Are you afraid?"

"Afraid? Who are you?"

"Think back," said Jack.

"Ah!" cried the girl. "It can't be you! You haven't dared come again!"

"D'you think it's as big a risk as that, lady?"

The door clicked. But it left her on the outside. She came straight down the veranda to him.

"Don't you know that the Vigilantes are watching for you? Don't you know that if they catch you there'll be no mercy?"

Jack Bristol laughed.

"I know all that," he said, "but it's worth the chance."

"Worth it?"

"Why not? It's worth a lot to hear you warning me of the danger. It means that I've got a friend in Culver Valley."

"I pity you with all my soul!"

"Lady," said Jack calmly, "I sure got to differ with you on that. Maybe you think it's pity, but it ain't."

There was an instant's pause.

"No?" asked the girl. "Then what is it that makes me warn you?"

"Shame," said Jack. "You're plumb ashamed of the way you yelled out and started them after me the other night."

"Yes," admitted the girl after a moment. "Perhaps that's it. They said—that you came within a hairs-breadth of being—"

"Yep. They had the rope hanging for me."

"If that had happened, I should have despised myself forever!"

"Why?" asked Jack.

"Why? Because you had done me no harm."

"Ain't there another reason?"

"Of what sort?"

"Lady, you knew that I wasn't Charlie Sherry!"

"What!"

"I say, you knew that I wasn't Charlie Sherry. When we rode through the dark talking, you knew that I was tolerable honest. Is that true?"

Again she paused, and finally she said, "They told me how you denied the poor old man when he claimed you for his son. Are you ashamed of your own father and mother, Charlie Sherry?"

"My father and mother never carried that name. But call me Charlie Sherry if you want. That makes no difference."

"I'm glad you confess your name!"

"I confess nothing," said Jack Bristol. "But no matter what you say, there's something on the inside of you that tells you I'm not a Sherry. You wouldn't be talking to me here otherwise. There's a sort of a sense in a girl that tells her when there's danger. And you know that there's a pile less now than there was when you were talking to Lee Jarvis, say, inside of your own home!"

"You've listened to us? You've overheard us again?"

"It's a right I have."

"A right!"

"They've double-crossed me and kept me out of a fair chance. I can't come by daylight, so I come by dark. Is there anything wrong in that? Suppose I hadn't come? I'd never have seen you turn your back on Jarvis."

"Do you think I turned my back on him? You have sharp eyes," said the girl curiously, "but I'm afraid they see more than the truth."

"Lady," said Jack, "when a gent takes a long chance on getting his neck stretched for the sake of seeing a girl, he most generally uses his eyes hard when he gets his look at her. I wasn't sitting here looking through the window at your face. I was looking right on through your mind and everything that went on inside you."

She started. But she came a little closer toward him.

"You're the strangest of all strange men I've ever known!" she said.

"That's because I'm telling the truth to you."

"And I think you strange for that reason?"

"Sure. I know the way men talk to girls. They act like the truth about things would be too much for a girl to understand. So they tell her just a little part of it, and dress the rest up in lies. I know, because I've done it myself!"

She began to laugh very softly.

"Charlie Sherry," she said. "I have to tell you to go away and never come back, for the sake of your own safety. But when you go I shall think of you a thousand times, I promise you that! You haven't been out of my head since I first met you last night."

"And you—" began Jack ardently.

"Hush!" said the girl. "I can guess that you were about to say something foolish. Isn't that true?"

"Whenever a gent lets go all holds and tells the truth about himself and the way he feels, why do people say he makes a fool of himself? Lady, I'm not ashamed. I came down here to see you once more. You've stayed in my mind like a picture I'd drawed myself. Ten times every hour I've been seeing the scratch and the spurt of that match Jarvis lighted, and then your face jumping out of the darkness, sort of scared and happy all at once. I came down here to see you once more, but now that I've seen you and heard you I know this isn't the last time. I'm coming again."

"No!" cried the girl. "If they caught you—"

Jack Bristol laughed.

"It's the greatest game in the world. I wouldn't miss a trick of it! There's only one thing in the world that's worth it, and that's Nell Carney; but she's worth a thousand times more!"

"Charlie Sherry," cried the girl, and the name brought him up sharply, "I shall never see you again, not if it means bringing you into such danger."

"Why," he broke in upon her, "if I know that you care so much, there's nothing that'll keep me away."

"But I understand," she exclaimed in a different tone, "it's only taking the chance that brings you here. It's the gambling spirit. Just as it was the gambling spirit that made Frank Stroud try to break into the bank and steal."

"And when Jarvis was telling about it," said Jack, "which did you like the most? Was it the thief or the rich man?"

"You have an uncanny way of looking into one's motives," said the girl. "And perhaps you're right. I remember poor Frank Stroud. His father was very well-to-do. And Frank was a happy, careless youngster. When Mr Jarvis crushed his father, Frank was able to do nothing but stay around and go to dances. And then his money gave out, and he disappeared; and here he is back, and ruined for life!"

"Has he done any worse," said Jack, "than Jarvis, when Jarvis smashed him?"

"Jarvis stayed inside the law."

"Nell!" called the voice of her father from within the house. "Oh, Nell!"

"Coming," she answered. "Charlie Sherry—"

"Are you going to stick to that name? Then, I'll do what you expect Charlie Sherry to do. I'll go down the valley for your sake and I'll let Frank Stroud out of the jail. Would that make you happy, Nell Carney?"

"You madman! You would be taken also. It wouldn't help Frank."

"I say, would it make you happy to see Frank free?"

"Happy as a lark. But if you go—"

"Nell!" called the father, and his footfall began to come down the stairs in the house.

"If I set him free, you'll see me again?" asked Jack.

"Yes, yes—I mean no—oh, what shall I do and say?"

"Say good-by," said Jack, "for tonight, and remember that Lee Jarvis will have the face of his father when he gets to that age. Good night, Nell, and remember!"

CHAPTER XVI

H E C A S T a circle around the little town of Dexter. Slowly, he sent the mare over the outskirts, jumping the fences one by one, sometimes riding a little way down one of the roads or lanes which focused in Dexter, and in short, examining at his leisure all the approaches—which were, incidentally, all the exits also.

And when that was done, he swung brown Susan around and cantered her straight down the main street along which all of the houses were grouped. It was a rash thing to do, when there were half a dozen men in the town who had actually seen him by the light of day, and while every other grown and armed man was on the lookout for him. But the very recklessness of it was his best safeguard. On the lookout though they might be, they would never dream of him actually galloping a horse through Dexter under the assembled noses of the Vigilantes so famous through Culver Valley. At least he went down that main street without interruption, even whisking through more than one bright shaft of light from window or open front door. And as he went he took stock of the town.

There was no doubt about the location of the jail with its barred windows and the bank opposite. A little further down the street he passed a stable full of livery horses. Then, striking out onto the open roads beyond the town, he quickly made a detour to the left and curved back behind Dexter again, for he had framed a plan.

Evening is the front-yard time in a village. The entire population of the town was gathered along the main street, gossiping, joking. Jack Bristol, coming in from behind, found it comparatively easy to pick the most likely horse in the pasture behind the livery stable. He left Susan, stalked and captured the horse, and tethered it to the fence. Then he ventured closer, slipped into the main stable itself and without difficulty secured a saddle and bridle. So equipped he returned to the horse in the pasture, saddled the animal, and brought it out through a gate.

Next, riding Susan and leading the tough pinto of which he had made a prize, he went down the length of the town until he came to a point opposite the flat roof of the jail. Here he tethered the pinto behind a tree, left Susan beside it, and started in toward the jail itself.

But the moment he began his approach it seemed that the entire aspect of the town had changed. All the life had hitherto seemed concentrated solely along the main street, but now it appeared that the silence along the backs of the houses was merely a symbol that the houses were filled with watching and waiting men, ready to attack him when he drew closer.

That illusion passed in a moment. A man began to sing in the yard at the back of the jail. He disappeared inside, banging a screen door which jingled behind him, while his song trailed away into the interior. Even a jail seemed to possess cheerful and homely attributes in Culver Valley.

Jack paused in the rear of a convenient tree to make his last preparations. Even as he stood there an inner door behind the screen door at the rear of the jail was closed with a heavy jar. It was a steel door, barred above, solid steel below, as he could see. The screen door on the outside was simply to keep out flies and mosquitoes. Seen dimly behind this door, the jail was a dimly lighted room, entangled with a maze of steel.

Jack sauntered around to the corner of the building and, leaning there, rolled a cigarette. He did not light it, but the rolling gave him excuse to loiter while he scanned the front of the building narrowly and the street nearby. Down that street half a dozen young men, just past boyhood, were frolicking not a full fifty yards away. They possessed man power enough to crush him and his attempt if they caught an alarm in time. The rest of the street was vacant. This section, the bank on one side and the jail on the other, might be called the downtown district in Dexter. And at this hour people were at their homes.

As for the jail itself, the cell of Frank Stroud could be easily located through the description which had been given by the elder Jarvis. There were three windows looking out upon the street, but two of these were large—ample for the admission of sun and air. The third alone was narrow and tall, though all three were heavily crisscrossed with bars. But only that narrow one could open upon a cell. The others must open upon a central hall, or the office of the jail-keeper.

The observations of Jack completed in this fashion, he took out from his pocket a section of black lining cut out of his coat on the ride into Dexter from the Carney house. This he tied around the top of his head, having first sliced it across the front for eyeholes. He rolled the mask on the top of his head, settled his hat in place, and then stepped briskly to the door of the jail. A pair of young fellows strolled past as he waited, and when they paused his heart jumped. How small a thing was required to thrill the nerves when one defied the law! They went on again almost at once, and in the meantime steps approached the door from the inside.

Jack twitched the mask down from the inside of his hat. As the door swung wide, he jabbed his revolver into the stomach of a corpulent gentleman who stood gasping before him.

"Make this quick," suggested Jack, and slipping inside, he closed the jail door behind him.

So doing, he shut out from the street the picture of the fat jail-keeper standing with his arms thrust up above his head. He dropped the revolver back to his side.

"Get your hands down!"

The other obeyed. Every cell in the jail was simply an open-work of bars. The gleam of that gun might catch the eye of the half dozen prisoners who lounged here and there in their cells; for the Dexter jail was the depository of criminals for all of the Culver Valley. There might be a riot in a moment if they suspected that there was a jail delivery taking place out of which they themselves obtained no advantage.

"Go back to your office," warned Jack sternly, but softly. "Mind you, walk brisk. And don't try no queer motions with your hands. I'm watching you every minute. Step lively, old son! I'm right behind you!"

The fat man opened the door and led the way into an office at a table in which sat a wide-shouldered youth leaning over an open ledger.

"And about this McGuire; this G. McGuire that you've got wrote down here, Dad?" he inquired.

"Get me a pair of handcuffs," said Jack.

The words brought the other bounding out of his chair. He was reaching for his gun as he landed on his feet. Then he caught the glint of Jack's leveled weapon. For an instant their eyes clashed. Then his hands came away and rose slowly above his head.

"That's good," said Jack. "That's mighty good! We pretty near had an accident happening, partner. Get those handcuffs, Dad."

The jailer found them without a word. Jack brought the arms of the youth behind him and snapped the steel manacles over his wrists.

"Listen," he said, "I'm not going to gag you, but if I hear a whisper out of you, I'm going to come back here and feed you lead, understand?"

The other flinched and Jack, turning to the father, gestured to him to lead the way.

"We got the jail all peaceful, now," he said. "Just take your keys along. We'll have Frank Stroud out of his cell, old son! Just make that pronto, too."

A wave of the gun made the jail-keeper start ahead with a grunt of haste. His heels struck heavily on the concrete flooring outside and that sound caused two or three heads to lift and turn toward them from the cots of the prisoners. Then they rose to their feet. The word passed. In five seconds every man in the jail was standing erect. They had not seen the revolver, for Jack now carried it in the pocket of his coat, but they knew that something was decidedly wrong; the air was filled with the scent of adventure.

Straight to the door of the cell farthest to the left went the jailer. Inside there was standing at the bars a big, blond man in the very prime of his late twenties. His big hands were gripping the steel rods before him. In the lock of his door the key turned. The jailer stepped back.

"Step easy. Take your time," Jack cautioned the prisoner. "Come out here into the aisle beside me!"

"What?" queried the prisoner.

"Go slow—" began Jack.

But as the door swung open he sensed danger at his side and turned in time to see the fat man reaching for a gun. Indeed the steel of the barrel was already glittering as he drew it forth. It needed only the touch of his trigger finger to wipe the fat man from his path, but instead, he drove his left fist into the pit of the jailer's stomach. He fell, gasping and wriggling. Jack picked the revolver out of his hand and gave it to Frank Stroud, who now stood excited beside him.

That fall had proven to the other prisoners that it was a jail break that they were witnessing, and a chorus of low voices began calling:

"You know me, Stroud. Give me a word to your pal!"

"Kid, listen to me! I can make you rich. I've got a turn that'll fix you for life."

"Hey, black mask, for God's sake don't leave me here in the hole when—"

"Let's let them out!" exclaimed Stroud. "The more of us the better!"

"Let out nothing!" commanded Jack. "I'm letting out one man and I've got one horse for him! Now sprint for that back door. I think there's only a latch holding it!"

Stroud waited for no more. He lit out at full speed with Jack at his heels and as they ran the low calls of the other prisoners changed to yells and imprecations of rage as they realized that they were not to be saved. Yonder on the floor lay the precious, glimmering bundle of keys which had fallen from the hand of the jailer. It had only to be picked up and tossed to one of them, and instead of that the two were fleeing to a selfish liberty.

The yell of the prisoners fairly split the roof of the jail. And when Jack and Frank Stroud threw open the rear doors of the building, the sound rolled loudly out with them, while the fat jailer, sitting up on the floor, began firing blindly in the general direction in which the pair had disappeared.

CHAPTER XVII

WHEN THE two fugitives sprang out into the night from the rear door of the jail, it was like leaping into the danger of an unwakened hive of bees. For the shouts from the jail had not raised a mere scattering of voices from the village. Instead, there was a literal roar of excitement and anger, and every voice that shouted in response was running at full speed toward the point from which the alarm had issued.

A frightened oath from Stroud asserted his alarm. When they reached the tree where the two horses were tethered, he flung himself into the saddle upon the pinto and plunged away at full speed. Quirt and heels drummed or lashed the flanks of the poor pinto until the durable little cowpony was throwing its head high in fear and bewilderment. Jack Bristol, ranging alongside at the effortless gallop of brown Susan, saw that his companion was wearing out his horse without even getting the full speed for a short distance out of the animal.

"Hold him in," he cautioned Stroud. "Let him hit his own gait. You're running him into the ground, partner."

Another oath answered him. "Hold him in? Why, you fool, they'll have a dozen racers on our heels in a minute. They'll run us ragged inside of two miles!" He added, "Listen! There they start. Good God, they must of been waiting for us all the time!"

As he spoke, there was a fresh outburst of shouts behind them, and then a shrill and wailing cry.

"That's Lee Jarvis, damn him!" groaned Frank Stroud. "That's Lee Jarvis on his hunter."

"What?"

"He's got a thoroughbred. Goes like the wind. We're done for. Jarvis and the rest must of been waiting for this to happen."

Even while he complained in his terror, he beat at the pinto, wrenching at the poor beast's mouth because it was incapable of a greater burst of speed, and every wrench, of course, helped to stop the cowpony.

They were flying down the Culver River road, now, and close behind them a gun barked; someone had fired at a shadow. That shot proved how close the danger stepped on their heels, however. And Frank Stroud fell into another fury of quirting. Finally, in disgust, Jack reined close.

"Look here," he said, "you see this mare I'm riding?"

"I see it. She's lightning on wheels. Lord, Lord, what a stride!"

"She'll beat the best they have behind her," said Jack. "She'll beat any of 'em if you'll ride her straight ahead and not start feeding her the whip. Go gentle with her and she'll break her heart for you."

"For me?"

"I mean it, Stroud. I gave a promise that I'd get you out of this and I'm going to do it."

"Man alive—!" began Frank Stroud.

"We'll change horses. Mind you, make it a quick change. Then you ride straight down the road. When you get into my saddle you'll find a rifle in the case. Don't use that gun shooting at men. You promise me that?"

"I do."

"One other thing, Stroud. When you get through with that hoss, tonight, ride her up through the mountains after you've shook off the Vigilantes. And leave her up at Hank Sherry's cabin. Then you can strike away through the mountains, and going north you'll make better time on foot than they could make if they lit out after you on hosses. Is that all clear?"

"All clear, partner."

"If you don't leave that mare the way I say, why, Stroud, I'll find you in the end and tear your heart out!"

"Partner, if I don't do what you tell me to do, I'm the worst hound that ever lived. But if you take this damned pinto, what's going to become of you?"

"I'm going to play a game, that's all. I'm going to take a chance and win out. Don't you start worrying about me, son! Here we are. Now change!"

They drew rein in unison, and like practised horsemen, bounded to the road and up again into the opposite saddles. Before them was a dark lane, where the trees from either side wound their branches together above the way and made a solid canopy.

"Ride like hell," said Jack. "Just let the reins hang. She'll take care of the rest. She can jump any fence you come to. She's as sure-footed as a goat! And forget that you got a whip!"

This last advice was called after Frank Stroud, for the mare, once given her head, darted away to a lead of a dozen lengths in hardly as many seconds. She was fading away into the shadows almost at once. At the same time, the leaders of the Vigilantes entering the tunnel under the trees, set up a tumult of shouts and haloos as they heard the pounding of the hoofs of their quarry so short a distance ahead.

Jack Bristol saw, at once, that the pinto could not live for ten minutes ahead of this pace. And he ducked the cowpony to the side and brought him up short behind a tree trunk. It made by no means a complete screen to an entire horse and rider. He could only hope that the posse, plunging headlong after the heels of brown Susan, would never think of glancing to the side.

It was on this hope that he had dared to make the exchange of horses with Frank Stroud. Brown Susan with no great effort should be able to shake off the best horses of the Vigilantes. So there was no harm in letting the bulk of the pursuit thunder on after her. So he waited, pressing the pinto closer to the broad trunk of the tree, and leaning in the saddle, so that he could look around it and survey the hollow way.

The posse passed him in a rush of thundering hoofs, one flying horse bounding in the lead—that must be Lee Jarvis on his hunter—and then half a dozen riders on mounts which were only a whit less fast. That was the first flight of the pursuit. Behind came others. And still more followed. Forty armed horsemen were rushing on the heels of brown Susan. And at the sight Jack Bristol's heart leaped with envy. If he were only on the back of the matchless mare, he would make a mock of these fellows and their pride. He would play with them. No doubt the thoroughbred could walk around Susan on a straightaway, but over rough going and through the wear and tear of half a dozen miles of hunting, the indomitable strength and courage would begin to tell. But the pinto? Against such speed he had not a chance!

The last of the hunt rushed past. And then, as he reined the pinto back, the cowpony stumbled, snorted, recovered his feet.

That slight noise was a tragedy. It had caught the ear of the last of the riders, and now the fellow, with a shout to his companions in the lead, swerved his horse around and came rushing back. So much Jack waited to see, and he saw, also, that other distant horsemen were swinging their mounts around. There were ample numbers for two hunts, this day.

As for Jack, he sent the pinto bolting through the woods, which stretched before him. There, at least, his training enabled him to put the fast roadsters of the others to shame. Accustomed to dodging hither and thither through the roundup at the heels of an agile calf, the pinto darted through the forest like a football half-back down a broken field.

A tumult of curses and shouts to the rear announced that the section of Vigilantes which had taken up this newer and hotter trail was driving ahead along it in spite of obstacles. Then the pinto came out onto a broad and smooth meadow. But Jack

Bristol cursed both the extent and the smoothness. These were just the things the well-mounted men behind him wanted.

He cut along the edge of the woods for a short distance and then twitched the pinto about and put him into the woods again. Would they hear him? Yes, he had fallen into a stretch of underbrush which set up a huge crackling, and when the Vigilantes came out into the open where their ears were not crammed by the racket which their own horses set up, they caught the noise at once and came after him with a cheer.

But they lost ground on that maneuver. They lost still more heavily in the second passage of the woods. But when Jack came onto the main river road once more, he knew there could be no more dodging back and forth among the trees. They would leave a guard on the outside and the inside of the grove, after this, and he would be running his head into a trap if he attempted to weave back and forth.

So he rattled off down the road at a round pace, never putting the pinto to his full speed, but keeping just inside it at a gait which the honest little horse could maintain for a great length of time. Would it be fast enough to hold off the flying Vigilantes, now that their own mounts had lost the keenest edge of their speed during the first brush?

He turned, as soon as he was clear of the trees, into the first rough field. He struck ploughed ground and gave it his blessing. Here the pinto was at home and the thoroughbreds and half-breds which the posse bestrode could break their proud hearts fretting through the heavy going. The pinto took it as a matter of course, laboring cheerfully ahead with pricking ears for which Jack's heart went out to him.

Then, looking behind, he saw the vanguard of the enemy take the fence with a rush. Lee Jarvis had taught his companions the pleasure of jumping, and now they rode as to a hunt. They had spied their quarry actually jogging at a trot in the semi-distance of the moonlight. And they went for him with wild yells of pleasure. Hunting? Yes, and the fox hunt was nothing compared to the man-trail!

Jack looked back anxiously. He had not covered any great distance on that ploughed ground. Would it be an efficient barrier against the pursuit, even for a little time?

He saw the leaders strike the soft dirt. It made them flounder. It stopped them up almost as though they had struck a stone wall. A trot, as all men know, is the thing for soft ground; a walk, of course, is even better. But who could keep a horse back to a trot when a quarry was actually in sight? Not these youthful Vigilantes now that they could see their man.

They sent their horses ahead at a round gallop, though at what prodigious cost of strength and wind to their mounts, who could say? They gained rapidly, to be sure. They gained so far on the trotting pinto, that their leaders opened fire with revolvers. But it was impossible to fire with any accuracy from the backs of horses pitching along through ploughed ground. And the pinto went scatheless.

Beyond, he passed through an open gate and onto firm ground, and now he loosed the rein and let the pinto fly away at full speed. Every instant placed yards of precious ground between him and the posse. And they, seeing what had happened, with furious shouts spurred their mounts over the intervening stretch of the ploughed ground. They reached the compacted soil quickly enough, but they reached it with winded, exhausted horses. The first sprint out of Dexter down the road had been enough to set their lungs laboring. The labor through the trees had been an added burden. And now this crossing the ploughed ground had exhausted most of them. It was like trying to sprint uphill.

They galloped across the level and easy ground beyond, but the spring was gone from their striding. They gained slowly for the first mile. Then, as the pinto struck into the first of the rolling hills, the bigger horses behind him began to stop. The fact that they were entirely spent was proved by the beginning of heavy fire from the Vigilantes. And now the pinto began to gain rapidly, putting the yards behind him hand over hand. Safety was only the matter of another mile, at the most, before the beaten posse gave up the trail or else merely jogged on, entirely disheartened.

The older heads among the posse seemed to realize this, for now half a dozen of them stopped their horses altogether, dropped to the ground, and uncasing their rifles began to drop bullets around the fugitive. Revolver fire from the back of the running horse was one thing. Rifle fire from a rest was quite another. Jack Bristol began to weave the galloping little pinto back and forth, back and forth like a dancer, and then, in mid-stride, the poor pinto was struck to the earth with a bullet through his head.

Jack Bristol was flung head over heels. He rose with his head spinning. It seemed to his dazed brain that enemies were rushing upon him from every corner of the compass. Then he ran for a circle of rocks which crowned the nearest hill.

CHAPTER XVIII

"MY NAME," said the brown-faced stranger, "is
Charlie Ganton. I been trailing this way to find a
gent named Jack Bristol, riding on a brown mare that's called
Susan—the slickest thing in the line of hoss-flesh that I ever
seen!"

"I ain't seen him pass this way," said Hank Sherry, after a
moment of due thought. "Come in and rest yourself while I fix
you up a snack for breakfast. Nope, I ain't seen your man Bristol!"

Charlie Ganton threw his reins and dropped to the ground.
He stretched himself, and then gave his body a violent shake.
The sun was newly up. The mountain chill and the mountain
freshness was in the air.

"I ate at sunrise," he said, "and I ain't hungry. But I'll trouble
you for a cup of that coffee. It sure sounds good to me!"

And he sniffed eagerly as the fragrance of the vapor blew
out to him.

The coffee was duly poured for him.

"If I might be asking," said Hank Sherry in his most ingra-
tiating voice and manner, "might you of come far on his trail,
this Jack Bristol that you been talking about?"

"About a thousand miles," said Charlie Ganton carelessly.
"Pass me some of that sugar, will you?"

"A thousand miles!" breathed the mountaineer. "A thousand
miles on one trail." His eye grew cold and bright. "That means
murder, I guess. That sure must mean a murder!"

The other looked at Hank for the first time with a keen attention. For a moment he said not a word, but sipped his coffee thoughtfully.

"So's not to put you off on the wrong foot," he said casually, "I'll tell you that it ain't murder. And if you ever see him passing this way, you tell him that Harry Ganton ain't dead, that Harry's brother has been looking for him, and that if he wants to go back to his home town, everything will be hunkydory."

"Not murder," repeated the mountaineer. "And Harry Ganton's brother is out looking for him. And if he comes back everything will be hunkydory."

"Including the hoss," put in Charlie. "He gets the hoss, too. Because Harry allows that Jack pretty near raised that filly, anyways. It belongs to Jack by right of bringing up, he says. Though, speaking personal, I don't see how he figures it."

The smile of Hank Sherry was so wonderfully bland that for the moment his face lost half of its ugliness.

"He gets a hoss and he gets let off for murder," he repeated. "That ought to sound like good news to him. Yep, if I was to meet up with him, I'd sure tell him what I know."

"Look here," said Charlie, "if you got any queer ideas from what I've said to you, you might as well get over 'em right now. My brother is a sheriff and he's fixed me up with a start and what not to go up here as his deputy. I don't mind telling the rest of the yarn. There ain't any mystery. Harry got into an argument with Jack and they went for their guns, and Harry was the one that dropped. The boys give Jack a run for his money, but he got away on Susan. Meantime, Harry is getting well hand over fist and he figures that the only way he can make up to Jack for the long trail he's sent him on is to give him that brown mare. Though Susan would bring a thousand dollars or even two thousand out of more'n one man in Arizona!"

"Two thousand for a hoss!" breathed the mountaineer. "Well, that's a considerable price. You folks down that way must be made of money. Set down, son, and tell me about your part of the country."

"Just a minute," said Charlie. "How come this to be here?"

From the junk pile nearest the door he picked up a piece of leather twisted into a peculiar braid.

"How'd you get that?"

Hank Sherry took the thing and turned it in his hand.

"Don't exactly recollect," he said calmly. "Don't remember what that might of come from."

"H-m-m!" said Charlie, his eyes bright with suspicion. "Anything about it that looks queer to you?"

"Yep. I don't think I ever before seen a braid exactly like that one!"

"Maybe you didn't," said Charlie, "because the only man I ever knowed worked up a leather braid like that was the man I'm after now—Jack Bristol!"

"Well, well, well!" murmured the mountaineer, stroking his bushy beard while he wagged his head. "You don't say, friend!"

"I do," muttered Charlie Ganton, and finishing his coffee at a draught, he stood up from his chair and fixed a keenly suspicious eye upon Sherry. At length, as though not able to see in what manner the other could profit by keeping the whereabouts of Bristol a secret, if he knew, he turned toward the door again.

"Which way had I better be going?" he asked the mountaineer.

Hank Sherry pointed to the east, away from Culver Valley.

"Hit out yonder," he said, "and you'll come into some good cow country. If your man come up from Arizona way, most like he'd be pretty apt to want to get into the cow country again, eh?"

"Most like," nodded Charlie Ganton, and swung into the saddle again.

"So long," he called, and waved his hand, but before his roan mustang had taken half a dozen steps, Charlie turned abruptly in the saddle and surprised a complacent smile of triumph upon the lips of Sherry. The latter banished the pleased expression at once, but not soon enough. Young Ganton, his brown face now darkened with suspicion and anger, wheeled his horse and came straight back.

"Stranger," he said coldly, "you know something. What's up?"

"Me?" said Sherry. "Know something? How come?"

"Partner," said Charlie Ganton soberly, "lemme tell you this, the gent that I'm on the trail of is a wild one. He was always on the ragged edge of raising hell and doing something that he could never undo. Now he thinks that he's done a murder, and he's apt to do another if he thinks he's cornered. He's that tigerish kind that go to hell quick once they've started. That's why I ask you to put me onto his trail if you know it."

"Sure," said Hank Sherry. "I'd do it in a minute. I sure would hate to see a gent cavorting around raising Ned. I'd sure hate to see that."

And in spite of himself, his glance wandered toward the west, where Culver Valley lay beyond the mountains.

And as he glanced in that direction, it happened by rare chance that Frank Stroud came over the hill and showed against the horizon on brown Susan. But it was merely the exigencies of the chase and through following the easiest way out of Culver Valley that he had come toward Hank Sherry's house, not through a desire to follow his word as pledged to Jack Bristol. And when Charlie Ganton, with a shout of pleasure, galloped toward him, he drew up brown Susan and meditated flight.

For never in his life had he bestrode such an animal as the mare. She had carried him faultlessly all the night, she had baffled the best speed and the cleverest maneuvers of the hardest riders in Culver Valley. And he could not find it in his heart to give her up to Hank Sherry to be kept for the man who had delivered him from jail. As for the man who galloped toward him, he came alone, and it was Stroud's boast that he feared no one man in the world.

So he drew rein and waited. Charlie Ganton, in the mean-time, slackened his pace when he saw that the horseman was not Jack Bristol. He drew down to a trot and then to a walk, while the roan pricked his ears at sight of Susan and neighed an eager greeting. They had known each other of old in the Ganton pastures far south.

"Partner," asked Charlie, "where's Jack Bristol?"

"Never heard of him," said Stroud truthfully.

"Never heard of him? Well, then, let me put it another way. Who'd you get this hoss from?"

"I raised her," said Stroud. "She was foaled right on my ranch."

"Hell, man!" snorted Ganton in disgust. "Look at the way she and this roan hoss of mine are rubbing noses. Don't that show they ain't strangers? I ask you again, where'd you get this hoss? I know her as well as I know my brother. It's Susan."

"Look here," said Stroud smoothly, though he shifted his hand so as to bring it nearer to the revolver which lay in the saddle holster. "I've seen men that folks couldn't tell apart. And if that's true of men it's still truer of hosses. I got no doubt that you think the name of this hoss is Susan. But it ain't. The name of this hoss is Belle. I raised her on my own ranch."

Ganton drew back.

"Partner," he said, "I sure hate to do this, but I got to. I've come all the way from Arizona to find the man that's been riding this hoss. Here's my badge—" he showed a star pinned inside the flap of his coat—"and I got to arrest you, stranger, for appearing with property that looks to me like stolen property."

"Arrest me?" echoed Frank Stroud, and his laughter was loud, though he kept his chin down and watched the other with a snarling earnestness. "Son, you ain't got a chance. Get out of the way. I'm due on the other side of the mountains and—look out, damn you, keep your hand clear from your gun!"

"In the name of the law," said Charlie Ganton with no little dignity, "I arrest you for—"

"To hell with you and the law!" exclaimed Stroud. "Get out of my way or—"

They went for their guns by mutual agreement, it seemed. The weapons leaped as though recoiling from springs into their hands. Frank Stroud was a shade quicker on the draw. His weapon exploded. But Charlie Ganton still sat his saddle. At the last instant he had both stooped and twisted sideways, and the bullet missed that moving and smaller target. His own bullet, discharged a fraction of a second later, struck squarely on the shoulder of Frank Stroud, jerking him far around. The shoulder bones were splintered by the ball. Clasping his left hand over the wound, he toppled to the ground with a cry of pain, while brown Susan, starting back in alarm, pricked her short ears and sniffed curiously at him.

CHAPTER XIX

THE ROCKS to which Jack Bristol had run crested a small knoll and from this commanding position the on-rushing Vigilantes recoiled and scattered into a circle, shouting their joy at having run the quarry to the ground. While they rushed for positions of strategic importance, however, Jack was busy as a beaver erecting a system of fortifications. The great stones which were heaped upon the crest he pried apart and rolled into a rough-shaped triangle. In the center of this he could lie with a fair degree of safety. So he crouched behind the barrier as soon as it was raised, and waited.

It was the end, of course. He might endure a siege here for a single day without food or water, but on the second day he must succumb. There was only one possible hope for escape, and that was through a rush under cover of the night to secure a horse from his besiegers and then break away across the country. But to steal out through the night in the face of such a circle of hungry-hearted manhunters and with the young moon shedding light over the hills would be merely a form of suicide.

Presently he heard a strong voice calling across the night from the top of an overlooking hill.

"Hellooooo! Stroud!"

"Hello!" cried Jack. Of course it was natural for them to think that this was Stroud.

"I'm coming down. Will you give me a truce to come by?"

"Come on, then! No tricks!"

A man appeared, looking gigantic in the faint moonlight and came upon the hilltop against the sky. He came boldly down into the hollow and then climbed the farther slope to the edge of Jack Bristol's fortification.

"Stroud," he said at once, "the jig's up."

"Sort of looks," said Jack, "that it is."

The other exclaimed, "Who the devil is this? It ain't Stroud!"

"Why not?"

"I know Frank's voice. You're the other one, then? By God, it's Charlie Sherry!"

"How'd you recognize me?"

"We knew that one of the hosses we was following was your hoss. But it never popped into our heads that you'd swap hosses with Stroud. What happened? Did he take it away from you? And after you got him out of jail?"

"Sort of looks that way, eh?" said Jack.

"Sherry, what the devil possessed you to break into the jail and get Stroud out? Was he ever a friend of yours? I can't remember him that way!"

"What does all this lead up to?"

"It leads up to this, Sherry: Give yourself up and come along with me and we'll give you a fair and square trial and if there's a hanging at the end of it, it'll be a legal hanging, Sherry. Does that sound good to you?"

"Who gives you authority to offer me all of this?"

"They told me to say that to Stroud. It'll hold for you, too, I guess."

"Go back and find out."

So the other departed, but Jack Bristol knew beforehand that there would be no answer. The men of Culver Valley had too many things against Charlie Sherry. They had been balked by him once when he slipped through their hands; now, for half a night, he had played back and forth with them and only by sheer luck or a chance shot had they managed to come within striking distance of him. And now that they had him cornered they would finish him then and there.

He was right. The stranger did not return to renew the proposal in the name of the rest of the Vigilantes and when, a little over an hour later, a volleying of hoofbeats was heard in the distance, Jack knew that the rest of the posse had returned from their vain chase of Susan and had come back to join in the killing of Charlie Sherry.

THEY BEGAN to build little bonfires behind the hilltops. Now and then shadows brushed into his view. It was long range for a revolver, but had he wished to do murder, he could have dropped more than one of the youngsters whose shouts and laughter rang down to him. They were making a merry night of it while they waited for a chance to get their quarry. Once he thought that their noise-making might indicate a lax watch and he slipped outside of his little fortress prepared for a dash for liberty. But the instant he began to run there was a solid volley of rifles. And he leaped back into his shelter with bullets flocking thick around him.

After that it was not long before pink began to streak the east. And with the coming of light the bombardment began. Just north of him rose the highest hill. It looked down upon him at such a sharp angle that they could open a dangerous and close-plunging fire. They had followed his example and erected, with their many hands, an ample and strong barrier of rocks. Thrusting out the muzzles of their rifles through the interstices among the stones, they dropped slug after slug into the triangle of Jack's fort. Not a shot flew wild. It was a large target, and they had plenty of lead. So they amused themselves in fancy and freakish bits of marksmanship.

They chipped the points off the rocks. They placed their bullets neatly through the holes of his wall. They proved to him in a hundred ways that he had only to show himself in order to be riddled with lead.

He showed a small stick. It was only a streak of a thing to be shot at, yet it had not been exposed three seconds before the end was snipped off. He showed it again. Again it was severed, and the crowd on the higher hill yelled their satisfaction. He tossed a rock into the air and with a cheer the youngsters above him loosed a volley. That rock struck the ground unnicked. But the next one he threw was snuffed to powder when a bullet struck it. They had scarred and whitened the surfaces of the rocks on the farther side of his wall, but still they kept it up. Each one of them had a cartridge belt to empty, and each was doing his best to get rid of powder and shot. Yet it was not an altogether useless exhibition, for it kept Jack crowded into a corner, not daring to move.

The sunlight was beginning to slant and spill into his fort when he heard a sudden shouting of dismay, and then warning cries. Peering out through a hole in the wall, he saw Nell Carney galloping at full speed across the hollow, while a score of voices were vainly warning her away. To Jack Bristol she came like a hope of heaven to one damned. When she drew near, he rose to meet her. Of course there were expert riflemen looking on, but would they dare to draw a bead, no matter with what skill, when Nell Carney was so near the target at which they aimed?

They did not dare. There was only an excited and enraged clamor of voices. And then Nell Carney had reined her horse beside him and was commanding him, in a voice hysterical with fear, to get back into shelter. He did not stir. She dropped out of the saddle and stood beside him so that her nearness could more effectually shield him.

"Oh, why, why have you done it?" she cried.

"Because I promised you to get him out, and he's free now, I guess."

"You held up the jail-keeper. You gave Frank your own horse. Was there ever such a generous madman in the world?"

"Lady, not a crazy man, but a gent that did what he told you he'd do. It looks like I throwed myself away. But you see, it was only the luck that broke against me. They nailed my hoss with a lucky shot. They nailed that poor old pinto hoss that I was riding. And that was sure an honest hoss, if ever an honest hoss stepped. He worked like a trouper. Never let up till he had all of them fast-stepping hosses dead-beat!"

"And you spend your time pitying the horse you rode when— when you're in a place like this?"

"Nell!" cried a voice from the top of the hill.

Jack looked up and saw Lee Jarvis recklessly exposing himself and calling to the girl to go from the hilltop at once, for otherwise terrible things were apt to happen. Jack raised his hand, and the figure on the hilltop dropped out of view behind his barricade.

"Doesn't take soothing syrup to quiet him," said Jack, grinning at the girl.

"Leave you?" she answered the demand of Lee Jarvis. "I'm going to stay until they've promised to let you have law."

"You're wrong," said Jack, "you've got less'n a minute to stay."

She shook her head.

"It was I who brought you into this. And I'm going to stay until you're out of danger."

"That's like you," said Jack thoughtfully. "A gent could see that you'd be as square as that. But it don't work, lady. I'm not going to hide behind a woman's skirts. That's ten times worse than dying. You see? But before you go I'm going to ask you one thing: You believe me when I say that I'm not Charlie Sherry?"

"I believe you," she answered, with great tears glistening in her eyes. "Oh, I knew all the time that you couldn't be he. But the scar seemed proof. I knew all the time. For there was something which made me believe what you said, and not what my eyes told me."

"Then one more thing," said Jack, "whatever happens to me will you keep in your mind that Lee Jarvis ain't worthy of you?

Nell, I've heard him lie about a man that licked him in a fair fight. And a man that'd lie about that ain't worth his salt."

"I'm only waiting to face him alone and then I shall tell him," said the girl, grown stern and savage for a moment.

"And that's all," said Jack. "Good-by."

"I told you before and I tell you now, I'm not going."

"Nell, in my part of the country a gent that hides behind a woman is called the worst hound in the world. If you don't go, I'm going to walk down that hill right into their guns. I swear I am. I'll fight this out without a woman's help!"

"No, no!"

"I mean it!"

She threw out her hands toward him, then checked the appeal.

"I'll go back up the hill and make them swear to give you a legal trial. Will you surrender then?"

"When they agree to a legal trial, yes," said Jack, and swallowed a sardonic smile.

But the girl, with a cry of triumph, was into the saddle, and as he dropped back into shelter, she turned in the saddle and kissed her hand to him—in full view of all those armed watchers on the hill!

There was something so gay and so gallant about her that it stopped his heart and, raising his head a little too recklessly a bullet jammed the hat off his head and flicked away a lock of his hair.

And after that, the steady bombardment was resumed. There was no more heard of the girl. They had taken her by force and led her away, as he knew that they would. They had led her away and, new men pouring in every moment from the surrounding farms, fresh belts of ammunition were beginning to empty toward the little fort as though they actually planned to shoot away the stones to powder.

In the meantime the pressure of a new and even more terrible enemy began to be felt. It was the rising sun which, as it sloped up toward meridian, heated the stones until they were difficult to touch, while the direct rays scorched the motionless body of the fugitive. If he could have raised his head above the wall to meet the breeze, but then there were bullets waiting. And he must endure all the long day until night. What time was it now? Not more than ten, at the most.

He amused himself looking out through the holes among the rocks and watching the arrival of newcomers until, close to the intolerable heat of the noon hour, he saw a rider coming on a horse whose liquid gallop was vaguely familiar. Yes, all in an instant he knew that it was Susan!

Had Frank Stroud come to give himself up in return for the freedom of the prisoner in the fort? No, in another moment his heart sank still more, for he had made out the bronzed features of Charlie Ganton, who would add to the list of charges against him that of murder. After this he could expect no mercy, indeed.

And, suddenly, he decided that he had endured long enough. It was useless to wait until his last energy was exhausted. Better, far better to die while he still had the strength to die fighting. He loaded his revolver, saw that it was in good working trim, drew up his belt to the last notch, and prepared to rise to his knees, but as he did so, Charlie Ganton rode over the brow of the hill above. To lead a charge?

No, he came with his hand raised, and behind him man after man was rising and waving; they were even calling what sounded like friendly words.

He listened in a daze. And when Charlie rode up, he rose, hardly knowing what he did. He found his hand gripped in a strong grasp. He felt himself clapped on the back.

"By God, Jack," Charlie was crying, "I've come at a lucky hour. But the trouble's over. I've come to tell you that Harry is not dead. That bullet only sliced him across the breast, the lucky devil! He's not dead, and he's sent me a thousand miles after you to get you out of mischief. And he's throwing in Susan, here, for full measure to make up for the distance you've traveled."

The brown mare thrust her head between them and poked her wet muzzle into the face of Jack. He patted her between the eyes, but still he was dazed, too utterly bewildered to understand. Other men were coming. Was it a trick, after all? No, they could not assume such smiling faces; they were not actors enough for that!

"I've cash to pay the man who owned the pinto. And I've left Frank Stroud—the skunk!—at Hank Sherry's, that old fox. They can get Stroud and bring him back to the Dexter jail whenever they want. If they want to go the limit and hold you for breaking into the jail, I have a warrant here from Harry to arrest you on another charge for something you done first. But that warrant will never be served, Jack, except to get you out of this mess!"

And then the whole truth burst on him like a flood of light, not out of the words which he had heard kindly Charlie Ganton speak, but because he saw Nell Carney come galloping over the hill while Lee Jarvis rode down-headed in the opposite direction.

He saw her sweep into the hollow like a bird. He saw her spur at full speed up the slope again. And before the others she was before him and stood on the ground facing him and laughing. But all the while that she laughed the tears were coursing down her face.

"Oh, Jack Bristol," she cried, "I'm the happiest person in the world. Because you knew all the time that you were an honest man; but I could only hope it!"

"Nell," he answered, "I never knew until this moment that I would die an honest man!"

THAT WAS the speech which Charlie Ganton carried back to the southland; but it was a speech which the townsmen in Arizona could not quite believe. They are still waiting to see the name of Jack Bristol in a headline.

For that matter, so is Mrs Jack Bristol, but she expects to see her husband's name in print for far other reasons; for Culver Valley has decided that it needs a sheriff. The Vigilantes are a matter of the past. So completely broken is their power that Jack Bristol could bring old Hank Sherry back into the valley with all of his crimes and all of his sorrows upon his head. And there he lives by the verge of the river in a hut whose front door looks out toward the blue Culver Mountains.

M AX BRAND is a Californian who saw the West first in the central valley of the State, where the Coast Range ran low on one side and the Sierra Nevadas on clear days were green and brown over the foothills, and blue or glass-white above. He learned something of cattle and cattlemen among the great grasslands of the foothills, but he never was so deep in that Old West which is a golden legend to-day, as when he spent a few weeks with two old trappers near the Diablo Mountains, close to El Paso, in Texas.

Nick and Alec had fought Indians, ridden range, prospected for gold, made fortunes for others, and had never been able to spend all the wealth that had poured in upon their minds. Some of the glory of mountains and desert remained with them as a perpetual heritage. Nick, at seventy-eight, had a body bent and twisted by age; Alec at eighty was straight as a stick, with no visible sign of the passage of time about him. But Alec was apt to blame his inability to read upon a defect of his eyes.

They quarreled constantly. To Max Brand, Nick reported that Alec was just a touchy old idiot—who could not even read! And what is a man capable of when he cannot read print? Alec, with equal fervor, reported that poor Nick was not to be blamed for weakness of temper and mind, for, said Alec, when a man's body is bent his brain is sure to sag also! But in spite of their wrangling, the two loved one another with a perfect devotion. And the long tales which they told in the evenings, making sixty years of Western history breathe and repainting mountains and deserts, have never been out of the mind of Max Brand. Nothing is more vivid to him than the memory of the little shanty near the "tank," the small stretchers on which the skins of coyotes and bobcats were drying, and the wrangling voices of old Nick and Alec.

Max Brand has been a traveler for a great many years, from the Pacific Islands to the deserts of northern Africa, but when he searches for stories, he most often goes back to that shanty in Texas, and the voices of the two old men pour up in his mind. That is why Western themes generally have come off his typewriter during the last sixteen years. In fact, he has written more Western stories than any other author. He is forty years old, was born on the Coast, spent twenty-three years in California, and since that time has lived east and west in diverse parts of the world.

www.ingramcontent.com/pod-product-compliance
Lightning Source LLC
Chambersburg PA
CBHW072000170626

46813CB00005B/1953